# CHAPTER 1

"HEY, HOW MANY MORE are there?" Rey called from inside the *Millennium Falcon*. Large cargo crates were stacked tightly in the *Falcon*'s hold, and as the service droids loaded the containers, the orange-and-white astromech, BB-8, rolled around them, beeping encouragement and helpful instructions. As the droids settled the crates, Rey strapped them down, a precautionary measure in case things shifted during flight.

They never knew when they were going to have to fight for their lives. It was good to be prepared.

For the past few days, Rey, Rose Tico, and Poe Dameron had been gathering supplies for the Resistance. They'd traveled all over the Outer Rim, avoiding the First Order as much as possible, and although they'd had a few near misses, they'd made it safely to Fermic, a factory planet with air that stank of the nearby fuel refineries. Thankfully, this was their last stop. Chewie and Finn had been on a similar assignment of their own, and Rey looked forward to getting the supplies back to the Resistance and seeing her friends again. There was so much work to do, especially if they were going to stop the First Order.

And Rey was ready to get down to business.

"That's the last of them," Rose called from the bottom of the boarding ramp. BB-8 rolled toward her and then back up the ramp ahead of her, beeping happily to welcome the Resistance mechanic aboard. Relief began to overwhelm Rey, but she quashed the feeling. Their supply run had gone without incident, and that was always something to be happy about. But there was still a long road ahead of them. Rey felt like every moment that ticked by was another chance for Kylo Ren and the First Order to expand their influence, and soon there would be very little left of the galaxy that hadn't been conquered by the relentless faction.

She couldn't rest just yet. There was still so much work to do.

"So, should I fly?" Poe asked, returning from the cockpit. He gave Rey a winning smile, and she grinned

FOR MADELINE, MY FAVORITE PORGLET

back. She had to admire his persistence. He'd been trying to take the pilot's seat since they'd set out, but the *Millennium Falcon* was hers for now, and she would fly it, even if Poe was determined to try out the controls of the legendary ship.

Maybe she would let him fly after they got back to the rendezvous point.

Maybe.

"No, but you can sit in the copilot seat if you want," Rey said sweetly. "I'm always happy to have someone so capable navigate." At Poe's near pout, she smiled. "I like flying, but if I need your help I will most definitely ask." She didn't want to hurt Poe's feelings. She just wanted to fly.

"I like flying, too," Poe mumbled, but he didn't argue.

BB-8 gave a series of beeps, and Poe scowled at him. "It's not my fault the First Order blew up my ship!" Poe exclaimed. "It's just one of those things that keeps happening. Seriously, I wasn't even *in* my ship the last time it got blown up. It's just rotten luck."

It was a familiar argument. Rey suspected BB-8 kept bringing up Poe's blasted ships as a way of having a little fun at his expense, and she thought it was rather funny. Apparently, Poe didn't.

BB-8 beeped back and rolled past Poe into the *Falcon*.

"I wasn't saying she isn't a good pilot, Beebee. I was

offering to fly in case she was tired," Poe said, following his droid.

Rose closed the hatch after shooing in a few of the porgs that had taken up residence in the *Falcon*, so they wouldn't be left on Fermic, and turned to Rey.

"Do you think we'll have any trouble on the way back?" Rose asked. As usual, the mechanic's expression hovered somewhere between worried and thoughtful. Rey hadn't known Rose very long. The first time Rey had seen Rose she'd been unconscious, knocked out during the fight on Crait. But since then Rey had worked with Rose quite a bit, and Rey had found her to be a really nice person. Rey could tell that Rose cared about others deeply. She was always offering to share her meager rations or let someone take a nap on her cot. She was just a very considerate person.

Rey shook her head in response to Rose's query. "It seems like the First Order hasn't made it to this part of the galaxy just yet. We'll clear the atmosphere and jump to hyperspace as soon as possible. That should help us avoid any trouble."

Rose nodded. "Good. Trouble is definitely something we don't need. I wish Finn and Chewie were here. They'd be great. Not that you aren't—great, that is. But Finn and Chewie would also be great and, well, you know what I mean?"

Rey grinned and nodded. "I miss Finn and Chewie, too," she said, knowing exactly what Rose meant.

Rose blushed a little. One of the porgs chirruped loudly, a sound somewhere between a trill and a scream, and landed on Rose's head. She waved it away. "Not now, Dita. I'll give you snacks later."

"Dita?" Rey asked, glancing at the porg as it chewed at Rose's pant leg.

"Yes! I've named them all. Dita, Tessalie, Jord . . ." At Rey's incredulous look, Rose's voice trailed off and she blushed deeper in embarrassment. "So, about Finn and Chewie. You think they're back from delivering that bacta Poe and Finn got from Tevel yet?"

Rey shrugged. "I don't know. I hope so. We have a lot of work to do if we want to stop the First Order, and the sooner everyone is back, the sooner we can get started. Supplies are important, but so is stopping the First Order from hurting anyone else."

Rose nodded. "Agreed. But it's hard to fight when you're hungry and you only have an old Corellian freighter."

"Hey, that's my ship you're talking about."

Rose laughed and patted the wall of the *Falcon*. A few more porgs scattered at the sound, running deeper into the holds. "It's a good ship, but we'll need a fleet to take on the First Order. Anyway, I'm sure General Organa has it well under control. I'll finish strapping down the rest of the crates if you want to head up to the cockpit. Before Poe steals your seat." Rose grinned.

"He wouldn't dare," Rey said, laughing, but she left Rose to the last of the work anyway. The truth was, Rey was anxious to get back to her friends. Every moment they spent preparing to fight was one more moment the First Order could grow and consolidate its power. If the Resistance waited too long to strike back, it would be too late. Already the odds were decidedly not in their favor, and even though Rey hoped that everything would work out for the best, she was also worried—about her friends and about everyone who had survived the battle on Crait.

There was no telling what awful things Kylo Ren and the First Order would dream up next.

Rey entered the cockpit to find Poe sitting in the copilot's seat, a frown on his face. He was flipping switches and muttering to himself. He looked so utterly perplexed that Rey couldn't help but grin.

"Having trouble figuring out which switch starts the engines?" she teased, picking up a fledgling porg and moving it out of her seat.

Poe startled and frowned deeper. "What? No, of course not." He caught Rey's grin and smiled back. "Oh, ha, very funny. You and Beebee should start a comedy routine."

BB-8 beeped his support for the idea, and Rey's smile faded. "Seriously, though, what's going on?"

Poe shook his head. "I'm not quite sure. I was going to send a quick message to let them know we're on our way back, and there seems to be someone already trying to send a message on the channel."

Rey sank into the pilot's seat. "Do you know who it is?"

"No, but this is a secret Resistance channel. No one should be able to hear it except for Resistance members."

Poe flipped another switch, and the noise on the comm filled the cockpit. It wasn't quite static but something like scratching and chittering. It sounded like nothing Rey had ever heard before, but there were lots of different kinds of people in the galaxy. It could very well be from somewhere she'd never been, which was most everywhere.

"What is that?" Rose asked, entering the cockpit and sitting in one of the jump seats near the door.

"That's what we were just trying to figure out," Rey said. "That sounds like, I don't know, some kind of language."

"Not Basic, though," Poe said. "And most Resistance communications are broadcast in Basic."

"And encoded. I'm guessing this one isn't?" Rey asked. Poe shook his head, confirming her suspicion.

"Maybe they don't know that," Rose said. "Before I joined the Resistance I thought a lot of things that were actually wrong. Why not respond to them and see if they answer?"

"If it's missing the latest scramble code it could be a trap," Poe said.

"But what if they just haven't gotten the most updated code?" Rose asked. "They could be in trouble and desperate. We should still see who it is."

Poe looked to Rey, and she shrugged. "Seems like as good a plan as any. It really could be someone in trouble." On Jakku, there were a number of beings who didn't speak Basic at all, and while Rey didn't recognize the sounds coming across the comm, Rose was smart. Maybe she was on to something.

Poe keyed the microphone that connected to the transponder and said, "Hello? Is anyone there?" Rey noticed that he didn't give a name or tell whoever might be on the channel that it was a Resistance frequency. After all, they had no idea who might be on the other end.

As Poe had said, it could be a trap.

Everyone waited quietly to see if there would be any response to Poe's inquiry. Just when Rey thought that maybe they'd imagined the sounds as something more than the usual planetary interference, a voice cut across the static.

"Yes, yes! Hello! This is Jem Arafoot, from Minfar. The

First Order is attempting to set up a base here. We request immediate assistance from the Resistance. We need—"

The message cut off suddenly, and once more the cockpit was silent.

Rey looked to Rose and then Poe. Their expressions matched her feelings of confusion and surprise. From the corridor, BB-8 beeped merrily.

Rey nodded, her uncertainty melting away. "You're right, Beebee-Ate. We do need to help them. But we have no idea how to do that."

"By getting these supplies back to the main Resistance force and then checking out this distress call with help," Poe said.

"What if we don't have that kind of time?" Rey asked, thinking of the way the ships of the First Order had invaded Crait. "If they find a way to embed themselves on this planet, it'll be nearly impossible to shake them loose."

"Maybe. But how many First Order personnel are there? A hundred? A thousand? If there are too many, we could end up landing smack-dab in the middle of a losing battle."

Poe had a good point, but something in Rey wanted to go to Minfar immediately. It felt like the place she needed to be. Was the Force guiding her way? Since the Battle of Crait, Rey had struggled with trying to figure out what were her own thoughts and what was tied to the larger, more complex workings of that magnificent power that united all life in the galaxy. She didn't understand the Force, if anyone truly did, but even more frustrating was not being able to use it to fix everything. It wasn't like a blaster or her staff, solid and steady in her hands. Instead, it was a bit like trying to grab a damp slugill, slippery and unpredictable. It made her doubt everything, including herself.

And yet every wayward thought and every second guess made it even harder to reach the Force. That much Rey did know—which was all in all disheartening.

Still, Force or no Force, it was the right thing to do to stop the First Order and help the people of Minfar. But it wouldn't do anyone any good if they ended up trapped, too.

Rey turned to Rose. "What do you think?"

Rose fiddled with her necklace and then sighed. "I don't know. These supplies need to get back to the Resistance as soon as possible. But I know what it's like to have the First Order destroy your planet." Rose's gaze went unfocused. Rey had heard rumors about Rose and her sister's flight from their home planet, and it seemed as though she was reliving just a bit of that. "I hate ignoring any kind of call for help."

"But what if it's a trap?" Rey asked. She couldn't let go

of Poe's valid misgivings. She knew how sneaky the First Order could be. She wouldn't put it past them to create a distraction just to stop the Resistance before it could even get started.

"We won't know until we check it out. That's kind of the trouble with an ambush: you never know it's coming until you're in the middle of it," Poe said, running his hand through his dark curls in agitation.

"But that distress call said they needed help fighting off First Order soldiers," Rey said, considering as many different sides of the problem as she could. "*Fighting* the First Order. This could be a good opportunity to find some new allies."

"Or it could be a trap, like you said," Rose said, crossing her arms. "Ugh, this is so difficult."

"Welcome to the Resistance," Poe said with a rueful grin. BB-8 gave a low, sad beep of agreement.

Rey turned to the only droid member of their crew. "Okay, so we're stuck on whether to head to the rendezvous point directly or go and help. What do you think, Beebee-Ate?"

The astromech droid rolled back and forth quietly, as though he was pacing, and then beeped a long, solemn note.

"Beebee-Ate is right," Rey said. "The right thing to do

is to offer them help. Think about how we would feel if we were the ones waiting for help that came too late. We can't do that to someone. If it's a trap, we'll deal with it. But I don't think it is. That voice? That person from Minfar sounded really, really scared."

"So we help them then," Poe said decisively. "And hope that it isn't a trap."

"Should we call the rest of the Resistance and let them know?" Rose asked.

Poe shook his head. "Not just yet. Let's see what we find on Minfar first." The Resistance pilot had a thoughtful expression on his face, and Rey wondered if he was thinking the same thing she was: it would be better to ask for forgiveness after they helped the people on Minfar than to ask for permission they might not get.

Rey nodded her agreement to Poe's decision and focused on launching the *Falcon*. Going to help the people on Minfar was the right thing to do.

But then why did she feel so nervous?

# CHAPTER 2

COMMANDER BRANWAYNE SPIFTZ stared at the junior officer standing before him. Spiftz's gaze was steely, his pale face expressionless. His teal uniform was pressed, his boots shone, and his black hair was slicked straight back. The only indication of his annoyance was the small muscle under his eye that twitched every so often. Otherwise, he was by every measure a First Order officer, and no one would mistake him for anything else.

If anyone did, he would correct that assumption. Forcefully.

Commander Spiftz's pale blue eyes catalogued every single detail of the man standing before him, and it would have been an understatement to say that the lieutenant was lacking. Not a single crease was out of place on Commander Spiftz's uniform, and his black boots reflected the lights of the command deck, which had also been spotless up until a few minutes ago. Perfection was the standard, as it should be.

Which was why the junior officer getting mud all over Commander Spiftz's command deck had a valuable lesson to learn.

"Lieutenant Aderat," Commander Spiftz said, his voice calm even as his face shaded to a deep burgundy of barely suppressed rage, "why is there mud on your boots?"

The lieutenant, a pale blond boy who could've passed for a younger cousin of General Hux, looked down. His light gray tunic and matching pants were disheveled, but his boots were by far the grandest affront. Red mud speckled the shiny black material, and the soles were covered in a thick carmine paste.

"Sir?" Lieutenant Aderat said, the single word more a question than a sign of respect.

"You came onto my command deck to render a report looking as though you just came from the field," Commander Spiftz said, lip curling as he stood from his chair and walked around the terminals toward the junior officer. The lower-ranking officers at the flight controls suddenly became very interested in their duties, their gazes locked on their displays.

Commander Spiftz walked closer to the lieutenant, whose eyes widened with barely suppressed fear as he realized his error. "I-I came as soon as possible to render a report, sir," Aderat said.

"Yes, I can see your haste," Commander Spiftz said, gaze going past the nervous Aderat to the footsteps outlined in red mud across the gleaming black deck. "Render your report, quickly, and then see to your appearance."

Lieutenant Aderat swallowed nervously, and the sheen of perspiration on his forehead increased noticeably. "Yes, sir. As of dawn this morning, we, um, have not been able to locate the laboratory on Minfar. The resistance forces keep forcing us to retreat."

Commander Spiftz, who had been headed back to his chair, spun on his heel. "*What?* The Resistance is on Minfar?"

"Uh, no, sir, we don't think they're actually part of the larger Resistance effort that we've been tracking. These fighters are less organized. Just a bunch of local rabble, sir."

"And yet these disorganized fighters have managed to keep you from establishing a foothold on this backwater planet of theirs," Spiftz said.

The lieutenant's eyes widened as he realized he'd made

yet another mistake. Before he could respond, Commander Spiftz continued. "Have you been able to track where these local rabble are holed up?"

"Um, no, sir. They just . . . disappear."

Commander Spiftz raised an eyebrow and took a menacing step closer to his subordinate. "They disappear?"

"Yes, sir."

Commander Spiftz laughed, the sound ugly and not at all amused. "What, are you suggesting that you're fighting a bunch of Jedi, able to *project* themselves from place to place like Luke Skywalker?" It was clear from Spiftz's tone that he didn't believe the Skywalker story, and what self-respecting First Order officer would? The Force was a myth, no more real than the supposedly terrible powers of Lord Vader. It was just another story told to keep unruly children in line. No matter what other First Order officers might believe, Spiftz was a man of intellect. He didn't believe in the Force, and he didn't believe that his junior officer could be such a fool.

Aderat stammered out some worthless excuse, his face growing alarmingly red. Spiftz waved his hand.

"Enough, Lieutenant. I find I have no more patience for your ineptitude. You are dismissed."

The lieutenant nodded and beat a hasty retreat from the command deck.

As soon as the man had disappeared from sight, Commander Spiftz turned to a lieutenant with warm brown skin and close-cropped curls. "Lieutenant Nivers."

The woman jumped to attention, her seat spinning from the force of her movement. "Yes, sir!"

"Congratulations, Lieutenant. I'm promoting you to expeditionary forces. Please tell Lieutenant Aderat he is relieved of duty. He can return to scrubbing pots in the galley. You are now in charge of the force on Minfar."

Nivers's eyes widened in abject terror, but then her expression steeled and she gave a short nod. "I will not let you down, sir," she said, before turning on her heel and departing the same way Aderat had.

"You know the girl has no idea how to lead any kind of ground force, Branwayne. She's a strategy analyst, not a stormtrooper."

"And if she fails, someone else will step forward to take her place, just as she did with Aderat."

Commander Spiftz looked over at Professor Glenna Kip. A tall, willowy woman, not quite human based on the greenish tint of her skin and the tiny scales that covered her face but also not any species Commander Spiftz had encountered in his years of military service. A gold-and-green scarf covered her head, and golden swirls marked her high cheekbones and outlined her eyes. That provided an odd counterpoint to her white smock, which seemed odd compared with the uniforms of the First Order. Whether the golden markings on the professor's skin were makeup or natural to her people, Spiftz didn't know. He also didn't care. His relationship with the scientist was purely professional, and he valued her technical insight more than her appearance.

Professor Glenna Kip was no First Order officer, but she was highly intelligent and worth every credit she was paid.

She'd been the one to ask him to lead this mission to a forgotten sector of the galaxy. Of course, she was not the one who mentioned that there were experimental laboratories on Minfar. That had been Commander Janson Hidreck, Branwayne's former friend and current adversary. When Hidreck had been assigned a Star Destroyer, Commander Spiftz had been jealous. *He* was the one who deserved to command such a mighty ship, not her.

Getting approval for a mission to Minfar hadn't been easy. Most of the other officers had laughed at Commander Hidreck's stories of forgotten tech on a far-off planet and the Echo Horn, a legendary weapon like no other. Hidreck's father had been a scientist in the labs long ago, so she was the logical choice to head the mission, but Glenna Kip had pulled Spiftz aside and convinced him it should be him, not Hidreck.

And he'd agreed—not because the stories Hidreck told sounded true; they sounded like farfetched fairy tales, like those silly stories of Lord Vader and the Force. But Glenna Kip was far older than she looked, and she had made a compelling argument. There were rumors she'd done work for the Empire back before the New Republic, although Spiftz doubted that the vaunted Empire ever would have let a nonhuman near one of its labs. But the scientist was incredibly knowledgeable, and the intel seemed like it was at least worth investigating.

Even if Hidreck was the one who had brought up the matter first.

Besides, Commander Spiftz knew to seize an opportunity when one presented itself, especially if it would give him a chance to show up his rival.

So he'd managed to secure a light cruiser, the *Ladara Vex*, complete with a crew, fifty stormtroopers, and nearly a full squadron of TIE fighters. It wasn't much, but it should've been enough to subdue whatever primitive forces occupied Minfar, a place that had no visible infrastructure and no history of any kind of culture. And yet there they were, several days after settling into orbit around the green-and-red planet, without even a hint of a base established on the planet's surface.

"Do you have anything for me, Madame Kip?" Spiftz

asked. "I do believe I requested an update on the possible location of the Imperial laboratories."

"*Professor* Kip," the woman corrected, her words firm even though her tone was mild. "Yes, I do have new information on Minfar." She smiled slightly. "Can you spare a moment?"

"Anything to ensure the mission's success," Commander Spiftz said, following Glenna as she wound her way between flight terminals toward her laboratory.

Commander Spiftz was almost to the doorway leading to the main corridor when one of the techs called out: "Commander Spiftz, we have an unidentified ship that just came out of hyperspace nearby."

Commander Spiftz waved a dismissive hand. "There's absolutely no reason anyone should be in this sector. It's probably just a lost freighter. Send a couple of TIE fighters after it until I return."

Commander Spiftz followed Glenna Kip out of the command bay, giving the random ship not a single additional thought.

# CHAPTER 3

THE *FALCON* CAME OUT of hyperspace with a slight jolt, jostling Poe awake. A porg flew off his head, and he ran his fingers through his hair to make sure it hadn't left a nest behind. Below him, BB-8 beeped merrily, and Poe stretched out and yawned.

"It was just a small nap, and yes, I slept fine." As an X-wing pilot, Poe had learned long ago that being able to sleep whenever, wherever was a huge benefit. Disaster had a way of sneaking up on you, and being well rested was always a plus.

Poe yawned once more, and just as he finished rubbing sleep out of his eyes, proximity sensors began beeping—loudly.

Rey rushed into the cockpit, taking the pilot's seat. "What's going on?"

"That's what's going on," Poe said, pointing at the four TIE fighters approaching rapidly.

BB-8 beeped in dismay, and Rey strapped herself in. "I guess the call for help wasn't a trap after all."

"Or it was, and this is the welcoming committee," Poe said.

"Maybe they just want to talk it out?" she joked.

The TIE fighters fired on them without warning, and Rey quickly maneuvered the *Falcon* out of the way of the blasts. Poe gripped his harness and held on until the ride smoothed out a bit. A few of the porgs inside the cockpit fled with a chorus of dismayed trills, their wings beating as they flew to less chaotic spaces.

"I think that's a no," Poe said wryly.

"What's going on?" Rose said over the intercom. "I'm trying to give this engine a tune-up and we're jumping all over the place."

"We've got company of the First Order variety. Rose, get to the top gun. Poe, can you grab the belly gun?"

Poe opened his mouth, and Rey stopped him by holding up her hand. "I can handle the flying," she said.

"I was just going to offer," Poe said, throwing her a winning smile before dashing down the corridor toward the gun bays. BB-8 beeped a reprimand after him, but he ignored the droid. Poe was too happy to be back in action to care much about the rebuke. Supply runs were okay, but blowing things up was even better.

Poe liked explosions, especially when the First Order was on the receiving end.

He really, really missed his X-wing.

The *Falcon* tilted suddenly, throwing Poe against the wall of the corridor.

"Sorry!" Rey called over the intercom. "We're going to have to start firing back or things are going to get very ugly."

"On it!" Rose called.

The sound of the top gun firing filled Poe with a sense of relief. He made his way to the ladder that led to the gun bays, gripping each side and sliding rather than stepping down the rungs. In less than two seconds he sat in the ventral gunner's seat and strapped in. The gun took a few moments to warm up, and then two of the TIE fighters appeared on his screen.

"Rey, can you take them on a bit of a chase?" Poe asked. "I don't have a clear shot."

"Yep. There's an ice ring a little ways away," Rey said. "Looks like there's some decent cover in there. I can try and make a run for it. But I don't know if they'll follow."

"Oh, they'll follow," Poe said with a grin. "If there's one thing the First Order likes, it's a fight."

"Why do you sound so happy about this?" Rose asked.

"Because every day we get to hurt them a little bit is a good day," Poe said, firing at one of the TIE fighters as it came too close. The shots missed, and Poe watched the TIE fighter speed by. The enemy ships were flying so much faster than the *Falcon*. Poe and his friends were going to have to get creative. He hoped Rey could maneuver the ship in a way the First Order didn't expect, opening up a few shots.

"All right, hold on," Rey said.

The *Falcon* tilted sharply to the right as Rey began a zigzagging approach to the ice ring. On Poe's display the TIE fighters followed, their turns faster than but not nearly as controlled as Rey's. One of the TIE fighters tried to overcompensate, and Poe fired as the targeting system locked on. Through the gun window, he saw the TIE fighter explode in shades of red and white, the display making Poe's heart glad.

"Got him!" Rey shouted in approval, and Poe had just enough time to whoop before the *Falcon* shuddered and shook.

"And it looks like one of them got us, as well," Rose said.

Poe sighed. It was always something.

The *Falcon* tilted once more, this time to the left. Poe tried shooting at the TIE fighters, but their turns were more controlled now, and the targeting system refused to lock.

"Yah!" Rose shouted from the nearby bay, and another explosion echoed dully through the *Falcon*. "I got one. You're getting rusty, Poe."

"What?" Poe exclaimed, his chair swiveling as the targeting system tried to lock on to the TIE fighters zooming past.

"Come on, Poe! You can do it," Rey said over the intercom.

Poe gritted his teeth. He knew they were just teasing him, but he really, really missed flying.

The *Falcon* swayed, dipping this way and that as Rey took them through the ice ring toward Minfar. Poe's gun display was a mess of red lines and speeding triangles but nothing close to being a good shot. At that rate, those last two TIE fighters were going to end up getting the better of them.

The *Falcon* lurched, explosions echoing through the ship as the TIE fighters fired on them. There were heavier thuds, as well, as Rey steered them into several chunks of ice. They began to spin, and Poe gripped the gun controls tightly. A porg flew past, screeching in dismay as it tried to account for the chaotic motion of the ship. "What are we doing, Rey?" he called, a tendril of worry filtering through his bravado.

"I just lost power to four of the engines. I'm trying to get out of this ice field, but we're slowing," Rey said. There was worry in her voice, too.

"Poe, you cover those last two ships. I'll get down there and check out the engines," Rose shouted, jumping down from the gun bay. Poe took a deep breath and let it out.

Two TIE fighters left. It should've been like shooting bala fish in a tank. But the *Falcon* was swooping and diving as Rey fought to maintain control. Poe had flown an unresponsive ship before. It was no easy task, and yet Rey had somehow managed to keep them steady and clear of the TIE fighters.

Poe was impressed.

"Rey, can you double back around and give me one clear shot?" Poe asked.

"Doing my best!" Rey called. The *Falcon* tilted suddenly as the TIE fighters began to close in, Rey giving Poe the perfect angle to lock on to an unwary enemy ship.

Poe pressed the firing mechanism and was rewarded with a brilliant display of red and orange sparks flying in every direction as the TIE fighter exploded.

"You got one more, Poe," Rey said. "I'm going to kill the engines. Make them think we're done."

"Good idea," Poe said as the engines suddenly cut out. Poe watched as the TIE fighter blazed past, firing with reckless abandon. He hated not trying to take the shot, but if he wanted to make the TIE fighter believe they had no power he was going to have to pretend that he couldn't shoot, either.

The TIE fighter flew past once, twice. On the third time past, the enemy ship slowed enough that Poe had a perfect lock. This time he didn't hesitate, firing wildly. The remaining TIE fighter exploded, and over the intercom Rey cheered.

"Great shooting, Poe! I'm going to get us out of this ice ring."

"Got it," Poe said, climbing out of the chair and heading back to the cockpit. "We need to get to Minfar before we have any more company. I'm sure there are more TIE fighters where those came from."

"That's probably for the best," Rose said over the comm. "Because we're down to five engine units, and it's not looking good. One of the TIE fighter blasts hit the compressor housing. It's cracked and causing the engines to malfunction. The rest of the engines could die at any moment. The sooner we get someplace safe, the better."

Poe walked down the corridor toward the cockpit and tried not to let the worry he felt creep in any farther. If something happened to them, there were a lot of supplies that wouldn't get to the Resistance, and the last thing he wanted to do was let down General Organa again.

"Well, let's hope Rey can land us safely before those remaining engines go," Poe said as BB-8 rolled along behind him. There was no way they'd be able to outfly or outmaneuver another group of TIE fighters with only five of the nine final-stage engine units. And without any engines, they would be in a lot of danger. The faster they found the people who had put out the call for help, the better.

Before they were the ones who needed help.

# CHAPTER 4

COMMANDER SPIFTZ looked at the map projected onto the table and crossed his arms. Professor Glenna Kip's expression was serene, her wide blue eyes and pale green skin showing no discernible emotion, but Spiftz could tell she was pleased by the way she kept tapping the map overlay.

"You found these in the archives from the Empire?" he asked, still not quite sure where the plans had come from.

"My personal archives," she purred. "I have been a scientist for a very, very long time."

Spiftz turned back to the hologram on the map table. Minfar spun in a lazy rotation, the faint green and red of the projection nowhere near as vibrant as the planet visible outside the light cruiser's viewports. But the hologram was merely a point of reference for Glenna's plan.

"Your stormtroopers have been looking here, here, and here for the laboratory," Glenna said, blue spots of color appearing on the map as she spoke. "And so far, they've found nothing."

"These were the coordinates that you provided to us," Spiftz said, his temper fraying just a bit. Soon his superiors would be asking for a status report. He could not tell General Hux his stormtroopers had been routed by a local population that didn't even use blasters. He'd end up getting reassigned to a supply depot on Hynestia.

"Yes," Glenna said, dragging Commander Spiftz's attention back to the map and away from his possibly grim future. "But I was mistaken. Please understand, Branwayne, that the weapons development that occurred on Minfar was not an approved program. Most of the Empire had no idea there was any work even happening here. So the record keeping was not incredibly detailed. My maps are inexact."

Commander Spiftz straightened his uniform, touching his perfect hair self-consciously. The way Glenna Kip used his first name always made him feel a little uncertain, as though she thought him a child and not a commanding officer of the First Order.

"So, now you think we should target our efforts in a different area?" Spiftz said, peering at the yellow spot that appeared on the map.

"Yes. I found a document talking about an evacuation point for the research team, and this was the location given. I believe that somewhere in this area is the entrance to the laboratories."

"And just how certain are you?" Commander Spiftz said. He didn't want to waste any more time looking for the lab in the wrong place. He'd been promised a weapon like no other, and he was determined to have it.

"As certain as one can be. But I believe that I could be of more use on the ground, directing your troops where to look."

"Absolutely not," Spiftz said, not bothering to hide his disgust at the idea. "This is a military operation, and although your knowledge has proven useful, there is no way we could let a civilian interrupt or observe how the First Order runs a mission." Spiftz did not add that he also didn't trust anything or anyone not human. Regardless, she was not truly of the First Order and, therefore, was inherently inferior. Just because she was useful did not mean she deserved respect.

Glenna nodded. "Well, then I believe you have the update that you requested?"

"Not quite. What about the fauna of the planet? Are there any species down there that could be attacking my stormtroopers?"

Glenna Kip waved her hand and the hologram of Minfar dissipated, a number of figures taking its place. "The scientists working on Minfar had a fascination with the planet biome. It somehow factored into their work. They tracked three major populations, but only one was sentient: the Zixon."

The other two figures shrank in size while the third grew. The creatures had large, slender, diamond-shaped ears, and paws with razor-sharp claws. Their bodies were covered in thick green fur, not long and shaggy like a Wookiee's but shorter and denser.

"Zixon? What a funny-sounding name," Commander Spiftz said.

"Yes, it was apparently tied to a squeaking noise the creatures made when they came upon the team. The scientists document trying to teach the creatures Basic, but they were hopelessly inept at learning any kinds of languages. But here is information you might find to be of use: the creatures lived almost exclusively underground."

"Is that so?" Spiftz said, rubbing his chin as he considered that bit of knowledge. Lieutenant Aderat had said that the creatures seemed to disappear. Perhaps they weren't actually vanishing so much as hiding themselves away. An entrance to an underground tunnel would be a good way to evade detection.

"The stormtroopers need to look for entrances to tunnels, then," Spiftz finally said with a decisive nod. "If these Zixon continue to be a threat, we will neutralize them and then find the laboratory. How hard can it be to subdue creatures that cannot even learn Basic?"

Glenna inclined her head wordlessly, but Commander Spiftz was already thinking about how the operation would be a victory.

Success would mean a promotion, and Spiftz spent a moment daydreaming about being given command of a larger ship, of a more robust fleet of TIE fighters.

Oh, the order he could bring with more power. He could finally make a name for himself. If General Hux, a child with a complete lack of vision just blindly following the philosophies of his father, could command a *Resurgent*-class ship, the most fearsome in all the galaxy, why couldn't Spiftz?

The mere idea of it made his palms sweat.

Commander Spiftz's reverie was interrupted—this time not by Glenna Kip and her hypotheses but by the shipboard communications crackling to life. "Commander Spiftz, sir. We have a situation."

Commander Spiftz gritted his teeth and turned back to Glenna. "Send these coordinates to Lieutenant Nivers and her team."

"Yes, of course," Professor Kip said with an inclination of her head. Commander Spiftz wasn't sure whether she was being insolent or not, but he didn't waste time on the matter. He just spun on his heel and made his way back to the command deck.

As Commander Spiftz arrived on deck, chaos greeted him. Battle analysts sat at their terminals with looks of mild panic and horror, and a number of alarms beeped distressingly.

"What is going on?" he demanded, and everyone on the command deck stilled.

"The ship that we reported earlier, sir? It, um, just destroyed four TIE fighters," offered one of the analysts, his expression somewhere between terrified and resigned.

"How. . . . Did. . . . A. . . . Transport. . . . Ship. . . . Destroy. . . . Four. . . . TIE. . . . Fighters?" Commander Spiftz ground out each word slowly. He'd been away from the command deck for only a moment, and somehow those fools had lost a third of his fighters. He'd made it clear to his crew that his resources were very limited, and now he was down to a small number of TIEs.

"It's the *Millennium Falcon*, sir," one young analyst

blurted out, two spots of color appearing high on her pale cheeks. "The ship we detected earlier was the Resistance."

Commander Spiftz straightened, and a glimmer of excitement quickened his pulse. "The rebels are here?"

"We aren't sure," another woman said, clicking through several screens and giving the other analysts a long look. "What we do know is that it was a YT-1300 Corellian freighter, which is the same model as the *Millennium Falcon*. This ship destroyed the initial group of TIE fighters we sent out to investigate and then headed toward the planet surface."

"And you let them get away?" Commander Spiftz growled.

"They were flying erratically when they fled, sir," the young woman hastily added. "I, uh, we thought it likely they went to the planet to make repairs."

"Why didn't you send a team in pursuit?" Spiftz asked. His pulse thrummed in his skull, and he could feel his control over his temper weakening dangerously.

"We didn't want to waste resources just in case we were wrong about the ship being Resistance," she said, her voice barely a whisper.

"We are tracking them, sir," another analyst chimed in. "As soon as they land we'll be able to send a team after them."

Commander Spiftz sank into his chair, feeling opportunity shine its benevolent light on him. If he could deliver the *Millennium Falcon*, the rebels, and a legendary weapon to the First Order high command, he would be due for a promotion for certain. And not just a single rank, either. He might end up promoted all the way to admiral.

"Excellent, most excellent," Commander Spiftz said, steepling his fingers, his previous anger completely evaporated. The barest hint of a smile played across his lips. "Please send for Lieutenant Nivers. I do believe our plans have changed."

The rebels would have no idea what hit them.

# CHAPTER 5

R EY HELD THE SHIP STEADY as they bumped the rest of the way out of the ice ring around Minfar. The creaks and thumps coming from the ship made her wince. She knew the *Falcon* would hold together—it was a surprisingly resilient old rust bucket—but that didn't mean she wasn't worried. Her heart hadn't stopped pounding just yet, and her palms were sweaty on the yoke. Those engines going out in the middle of a fight was a bad sign, and Rey couldn't help but worry that they'd made a mistake going all the way to the edge of the known galaxy to help people they'd never met. It was the right thing to do, but sometimes doing the right thing led to nothing but trouble.

And didn't they already have enough problems?

As though it sensed her mood, a porg landed on the control console and cooed soothingly. Rey smiled tightly. "Now, are you Erci or Mady?" she asked.

The porg trilled in response.

Poe jogged into the cockpit and strapped into the seat next to Rey. He still wore a goofy grin from their battle, and Rey tried not to scowl at him. At least one of them was having fun.

"Are you okay?" he asked as BB-8 rolled in and beeped a similar inquiry.

"Great, just trying to get us to the planet without any further disaster."

Poe nodded and stared out the window at the star-studded inky blackness before them. "That was some really great flying back there. I'm sorry I doubted you," he said.

Rey turned as much as the seat belt would allow. "What do you mean, you doubted me? You didn't think I was a good enough pilot to outrun a few TIE fighters?"

Poe's expression turned contrite. "Yes, I know you're an okay pilot, but you even said yourself that you haven't been flying that long, just since you left Jakku. I kind of figured I was better at it than you, and now that I'm saying it out loud I realize how much that makes me sound like a jerk." Poe took a deep breath and let it out, his expression troubled. "I know you're a great pilot, okay? I just some-times forget that I'm not the *only* great pilot. And don't say a word about the First Order destroying my ships," he said with a pointed glance at BB-8.

Rey pressed her lips together and said nothing, but the porg on the control console screeched before flying away. She didn't know Poe that well, but his doubt in her abilities stung, even when he was apologizing for doubting her.

"Are you mad at me?" Poe asked.

"No, I just didn't know you didn't think I was a good pilot."

"Why did you think I kept asking to fly?" Poe asked, amazed.

"I thought you just wanted to fly!" Rey said. "You are a little bit of a control freak."

"What? I am not," Poe said. BB-8 beeped a reply from the corridor that made Poe scowl. "Okay, maybe a little bit. Either way, I was apologizing!"

"And I appreciate your apology," Rey said.

A dozen sensors began beeping, and Rey turned her attention back to the controls. Whatever was going on with the engines had also damaged several other subsystems, and the *Falcon* was not happy about it. They were clear of the ice ring, so Rey was able to send the ship hurtling toward the green-and-red planet in the distance.

Minfar. She just had to hope they could find a place to land before the remaining engines gave out.

They broke into the atmosphere with a bump, harder than Rey would have expected, and she didn't ponder why. The faster they landed, the sooner she and Rose could give the ship a once-over. Until then, she just had to focus on flying. And landing.

A dark shadow swooped past, lighting up a number of sensors, and Rey banked the *Falcon* hard to the left.

"Whoa, did you see that?" Poe asked, leaning forward in his seat.

"Yes. What was it?" Rey asked, her previous worry blossoming into full-fledged panic. Was it more TIE fighters?

But the shadow came back, and this time Rey was able to get a good look at it. A giant flying beast swooped past, letting out a primordial scream. The noise of it reverberated through the ship, leaving Rey's bones vibrating. The creature had two sets of wings—one black, the other white. What looked to be interlocking black and white scales coated its sinuous body, giving it a patterned look that shifted as it flew through the air. The creature was at least twice the size of the *Millennium Falcon*, and Rey's mouth went dry as the beast circled back around.

"Uh, Rey, does that thing look angry to you?" Poe asked, eyes wide.

"It does not look happy, not at all."

The creature flew right at them, and Rey moved quickly. She banked the *Falcon* so the monster flew past them.

"Rey, get us out of here!" Poe yelled.

"I'm trying!" Rey yelled back.

Rey didn't have much time to think. A heavy canopy of trees stood not far off, and she steered the ship in that direction.

"Where are you going?" Poe asked, his gaze on the thing chasing them.

"Those trees are pretty close together, and that thing is pretty big. Let's see how it does in the jungle."

Poe leaned back in his chair and gave Rey a slightly panicked look. "I said I was sorry I doubted you were a great pilot. That doesn't mean you have to prove me wrong."

That made Rey grin. "Hold on."

The *Millennium Falcon* tilted hard, BB-8 rolling this way and that as he tried to account for the rapid change in direction. The ship was slower than Rey would have liked due to multiple engines being down, but it still zigzagged through the trees, faster and easier than the creature chasing them could.

The intercom crackled to life. "Um, guys, what's happening up there?" Rose asked, her voice a little shaky.

"We're trying to avoid being eaten, Rose," Poe said.

"Oh, well, good to know. But if you keep pushing the engines like this we're going to—"

Rose was cut off as one of the remaining engines went out, and Rey gripped the yoke. "HOLD ON!" she yelled. The *Falcon* pitched and rolled, threatening to smash into the trees that pressed in from all directions. Rey managed to keep the ship from crashing into any of the huge green towers of the jungle. Just when she began to despair, an open space appeared.

Rey turned the ship toward the perfectly sized clearing, the *Falcon* landing harder than usual. The ship creaked and protested as it slid to a stop, and the restraints pulled tight against Rey's body as she was yanked forward and then thrown back.

In the quiet that followed the hard landing, Rey took a deep breath and let it out. "Is everyone okay?" she asked.

BB-8 chirped a positive and Poe groaned. "Great crash."

"That was not a crash," Rey said. "It was a rough landing."

Poe nodded and unstrapped himself. "Well, bright side: we did not get eaten."

Rey undid her restraints, as well. "At least something's going right. Let's go check on Rose."

They made their way to the engine room carefully, and when they got there they found Rose standing with her hands on her hips, staring at the seven sublight engines. Grease streaked her cheek, and her expression was somewhere between grim and annoyed.

"Are you okay, Rose?" Rey asked, and the mechanic nodded.

"I'm fine, but our engines are shot. We pushed them too hard, and now the compressor housing is *completely* broken, not just a little broken," Rose said, crossing her arms. "We're going to have to find a new one."

Rey sighed. "Well, let's hope our new friends can help. Otherwise, we're going to be here for a very, very long time."

# CHAPTER 6

THE *LADARA VEX* was a maelstrom of activity. Lieutenants barked orders as technicians ran this way and that, preparing transports for departure. The heavy sound of stormtrooper boots echoed throughout the loading bay. Commander Spiftz watched the activity with a satisfied smile. About an hour ago, the *Millennium Falcon* had landed on Minfar. In another hour Commander Spiftz and his full contingent of stormtroopers, all fifty of them, would be on the planet, as well. The *Millennium Falcon* might be a formidable opponent in a fight, but how much could it do on the ground?

Commander Spiftz would find out.

"Branwayne," Glenna Kip said, sidling up to him with her sinuous grace. "What is going on?"

Commander Spiftz couldn't quite keep the joy from his face as he turned to look at the scientist.

"The Resistance members and their ship, the *Millennium Falcon*, have just crashed on Minfar. I am sending a devastating force to confront them. I do believe this will be an even better outcome than we'd hoped."

Glenna's usual pleasant expression slipped, her thin lips nearly disappearing as she pressed them together. "The rebels are an unfortunate complication, but our mission is clear. We need to find the hidden labs and extricate the Echo Horn. It is, as you know, a weapon that has the ability to use sound to control any group that hears its call. To let such a powerful weapon fall into the wrong hands would be folly. We should do all that we can to recover it."

"And we shall, my dear," Commander Spiftz said, his tone clearly dismissive. "But first, we are going to capture these upstarts. Once we have them securely on board the *Ladara Vex*, we'll be free to continue searching for the laboratories. Do not despair. You will have plenty of time for research while we wait up here on the ship for the operation on Minfar to conclude." Commander Spiftz adjusted his black gloves, pulling them on more securely. He had no intention of going down to Minfar and living in a command tent. That was why he had junior officers. But he would enjoy watching the operation unfold. "This is a fruit ripe for the picking, Madame Kip. We would be foolish to overlook it."

Glenna Kip's expression didn't change. She still appeared vaguely disgruntled, but she did incline her head in acknowledgment, if not agreement. "*Professor* Kip. As you desire, Branwayne."

"Sir." A breathless technician ran up, his salute sloppy and undisciplined. Commander Spiftz gritted his teeth but said nothing. At least the man's uniform was orderly.

"What is it?" Commander Spiftz said.

"There is a call for you from command. It's urgent."

Commander Spiftz would normally experience a deep sense of dread at the idea of a call from General Hux, but not that day.

That day, he had good news.

"Patch it through to the command deck. I'll answer it there." The communications node on the command deck could be heard by everyone on the deck of the *Ladara Vex*. He wanted to make sure that everyone heard as he gave his report. It wasn't often that they had such an exciting development.

Commander Spiftz made his way through the ship, entering the command deck with as close to a smile as he was capable of. The command deck was sparsely populated. Disappointing. There should be more of an audience for such a tantalizing announcement. That was the problem with running a relatively small ship. The light cruiser seemed like a child's toy next to the Dreadnoughts commanded by General Hux. With only a hundred crew members, not counting the stormtroopers and TIE pilots, nearly all the shipboard staff had been assigned to the mission to find the rebels. The ship would be a veritable ghost town once the transports left.

This would never happen on a Dreadnought. Or a Star Destroyer. When Commander Spiftz was promoted, he would never have to worry about having too small of a crew again.

"This is Commander Branwayne Spiftz," he said, sinking into his chair.

The hologram projected on the communications node was not that of General Hux, as Commander Spiftz had hoped. It was instead Commander Janson Hidreck. Her stern expression caused Commander Spiftz to sit up a tiny bit straighter in his chair.

"Commander Hidreck," Spiftz said, not trying to keep the distaste from his voice.

"Branwayne, what is this nonsense I'm hearing about the Resistance operating on Minfar?" she said. The blue hologram did nothing to lessen the appearance of the deep wrinkles of her forehead as she scowled at him.

"It isn't nonsense, Janson. Four of my TIE fighters were just destroyed by a known Resistance freighter." Spiftz omitted that it might be the *Millennium Falcon.* If he suggested that, every ship in the fleet would descend on Minfar, and then he would get nothing: no promotions, no medals, just pushed out of the way so another officer could take the credit and the glory.

"A single freighter managed to overwhelm four of your TIE fighters? Just what kind of operation are you running there, Spiftz?"

He fought to keep the annoyance off his face and instead stared at the projection in front of him. "The ship is heavily damaged. I believe they are attempting to render aid to the rebels on Minfar," Spiftz said. So what if he didn't actually believe there was any real fighting presence on the jungle planet? Commander Hidreck didn't need to know that.

"Minfar is a planet without any kind of intelligent life, Spiftz. I've read the reports the same as you. In fact, I was the one who suggested the First Order conduct a reconnaissance mission to identify the possibility of lost technology on the planet, in case you've forgotten who got you where you are."

"And yet you mocked me when I decided to pursue a search for the lost laboratories."

"Because you wanted to launch a full-scale attack on the planet. The initial reports did not prove anything but that pursuing the possibility of a weapons lab on Minfar was a worthless waste of resources, which is why *I* abandoned my efforts to conduct a large-scale mission there."

"Funny, I thought you were asked to step aside so that I could lead the effort instead," Spiftz said.

Hidreck shrugged. "Remember it how you wish, Branwayne. It still seems as though you are creating this fantasy of it being a Resistance stronghold to justify your future failure."

Spiftz clenched his fists but did not respond. What a foolish woman Commander Hidreck was, to so blindly ignore what was right in front of her. She'd never abandoned her ambitions of visiting the planet; she'd just been thwarted because the command had decided to back Spiftz's effort instead. And now it looked as though the planet was even more important than previously thought. Minfar might not be a Resistance base, but there had to be a reason the rebels were there. They couldn't have just accidentally ended up in that remote part of the galaxy.

"Janson, as much as I would love to waste more of my precious time arguing with you, I'm afraid I have a mission to oversee. I have possible Resistance activity, and that takes precedence."

"Yes, I know. That is why I contacted you. Due to this latest development, the leadership has decided that Minfar warrants more attention than just your half measures. My Destroyer will be there to lend assistance in two days, once we wrap up our pacification efforts here. I figured since we were old friends I would give you the courtesy of letting you know."

"You're coming . . . here?" Commander Spiftz said, completely unable to keep the surprise from his voice.

"Yes. So instead of finding the labs and pursuing the rebels on your own, your job is to establish a base of operations on Minfar. And when I arrive, we shall pursue the rebels and the lost laboratories together. Don't look so startled, Branwayne. You only have to set up an expeditionary post. Even *you* should be able to do that in two days."

The hologram faded, and Commander Spiftz continued to stare at the space where it had been. He felt like he'd been punched right in the stomach. All his visions of glory and victory lay in ruins. Commander Hidreck and her stupid Star Destroyer would ride in and ruin everything. She would take credit for capturing the rebels, and probably for finding the legendary weapon, as well. Commander Spiftz would be left out in the cold, without even a shred of dignity, just another failure to his name.

Not if he could help it.

He exploded out of his chair and marched back toward the loading bay, ignoring the junior officers who dodged him as he went. When he took up his spot once more on the observation balcony, Glenna Kip gave him a long look.

"Is something amiss, Branwayne?"

"Prepare yourself for departure. Bring along whatever you need," Commander Spiftz said. "We are going to be heading down to the planet's surface, as well. I have decided to oversee this mission, personally."

A few technicians standing nearby overheard Commander Spiftz's declaration, and they scrambled off, no doubt to spread the word. Glenna Kip said nothing, only watched him with her inscrutable eyes, her green-skinned countenance seemingly unbothered. That was fine. Commander Spiftz had enough annoyance for the both of them.

He had two days to capture the rebels and find the lost laboratories. He would do it in one.

# CHAPTER 7

REY GRABBED HER STAFF and her bag while Poe strapped his blasters to his hips. Rose waited at the foot of the boarding ramp, her face twisted with worry.

"I hope they'll be okay," she said, gesturing to the porgs that had left the *Falcon* and begun to scratch at the red soil of the clearing.

"I suppose the worst thing that could happen to them is they get eaten," Poe said. At Rose's horrified look he shrugged. "What? They look delicious."

"Ignore him, Na-Ne," Rose said to a porg near her as it unearthed a bug and swallowed it whole. "He's just grumpy because he hasn't gotten to fly."

Rey smothered a grin and cleared her throat. "Are we ready?"

"Sure! But . . . I don't suppose either of you know which way we're supposed to go," Rose said, looking left and then right at the dense underbrush of the jungle.

Poe jumped off the boarding ramp and looked up at Rey. "Maybe the Force could tell you how to find our friends with the distress call?"

Rey pressed her lips together and shook her head. "It doesn't work that way. The Force isn't just a comm unit I can turn off and on."

"Maybe you could try?" Rose asked with a small smile. "This jungle is really thick, and who knows what could be out there. A little help from the Force would go a long way."

Rey sighed and closed her eyes. She reached for that part of her that always felt connected to life, to the galaxy and everyone in it. The connection was there as usual, bright and strong, and it made her glad. She took a deep breath and let it out, and then she sent a question toward that connection.

*Where are the people we're here to help?* she thought.

She waited a few long seconds before opening her eyes. Both Poe and Rose watched her expectantly, and Rey shrugged. "No luck," she said.

"Well, maybe we can try the secure channel again," Poe said.

"Don't you think maybe the First Order is monitoring the channel now?" Rose asked. "That's the last thing we want, the First Order knowing where we're headed."

Poe nodded. "Good point."

"So, how are we going to find this Jem?" Poe asked.

"Maybe Beebee-Ate has some ideas?" Rey said, looking down at the little droid.

BB-8 beeped as though he'd just been waiting for someone to ask his opinion and whirled off through the underbrush.

"Um, I guess that's a yes?" Rose said, running after the little droid. Poe took off after them.

Rey stopped just long enough to secure the boarding ramp before she dashed into the jungle behind Rose, Poe, and the merrily beeping BB-8.

The jungle of Minfar was nothing like Rey had ever seen before. Plants with red- and green-striped leaves covered the ground. The air had a sweet smell, and small creatures chittered loudly, falling silent as the friends hurried past. Here and there black flowers peeked out from beneath the huge leaves, which were large enough to block Rey's view of her friends if she didn't keep up.

"Hey, can we slow down?" Rey asked, using her staff

to knock aside a particularly stubborn leaf. She wanted to take in the landscape a little more, but running through dense jungle also seemed like a terrible idea. After all, they'd fought a group of First Order TIE fighters to get there.

"Rey's right, Beebee. Maybe you should—*WHOA!*" Poe was cut off midsentence, and Rey slid to a stop as he and the others disappeared from sight.

"Poe? Rose? Beebee-Ate? Where'd you go?" Rey walked forward cautiously, batting the giant leaves aside to find their trail. She was so busy looking up that she didn't look down. One moment the ground was there, the next Rey was sliding down a very long, dark tunnel. She clutched her staff to her chest as she fell, leaning back to keep from banging her head on the low ceiling. She tried to angle the weapon to the side to slow her descent, but the tunnel was made of hard, shiny rock. Spiky plants growing from the top of the tunnel gave off an eerie glow, and if she wasn't so busy trying to slow herself down it might have been kind of neat.

By the time she came to a stop at the bottom of the tunnel she had her staff up and was ready to defend herself.

"Rey, it's okay!" Rose said. Dirt smudged her cheeks and bits of leaves clung to her ponytail, but she grinned hugely. "I think we were supposed to find this tunnel. That's why Beebee-Ate led us this way."

Rey planted the end of her staff on the ground and took in her surroundings. Now that she was a bit less worried about fighting, she could see that they were in some kind of chamber. More of the spiky plants grew down there, as well, casting the underground world in a soft blue glow.

"It's really pretty," Rose said, head tilted as she took in the smooth rock walls and high ceiling.

"Do you think someone built this?" Poe asked, and BB-8 beeped happily in response.

"Beebee-Ate is right," Rey said, reaching out to touch one of the walls. "The rock is so smooth. Only water could have done this naturally."

"And the tunnel is really dry," Rose said. "But look at these plants. Bioluminescence, the ability of plants and animals to give off light. My sister, Paige, and I used to go exploring on D'Qar, and we found a cave full of plants like this once. She would have loved to see this." Rose's voice softened.

"Yes, this is strange. But also very pretty," Rey said, hefting her staff. "At least it looks like there's only one way to go." She pointed toward the far right edge of the cavern and the tunnel that led into the darkness.

Poe drew his blaster. "Okay, let's be careful. Not so fast this time, Beebee. We don't know what else could be down here, and the last thing we want is any unwelcome surprises."

BB-8 beeped in agreement and rolled ahead, his search-light a glowing beacon that everyone could easily follow. Poe walked right behind the droid, followed by Rose, with Rey not far behind. She kept her staff out, figuring it was her best weapon for the close quarters of the tunnel.

As they walked the glowing plants changed color, going from blue to yellow. Rey wasn't certain whether it was a way to mark the pathway or just a natural shift in the lighting, like the sun brightening the sky before setting for the night. The air underground was fresh and sweet, and as they turned a corner Rey got a whiff of something spicy and smoky that made her stomach growl.

"Do you guys smell food?" Rey asked, and Rose nodded.

"It smells really good, like pongol stew," she said.

"I really wish we'd eaten before leaving Fermic," Poe said, his voice low.

The farther they walked, the stronger the food smell got, until Rey's mouth watered at the possibility of finding the source of the scent.

Just when it felt as if they had been walking for a lifetime, even though it had only been a few minutes, the tunnel ended on a narrow ledge.

"Whoa!" Poe said, waving Rose and Rey back. BB-8 beeped in annoyance, and Poe shook his head. "I think you might have a circuit crossed, buddy. There's no bridge there. Just a bottomless pit."

Rey peered around Poe's shoulder, and sure enough, there was no way forward. The rock continued a little way past the opening onto an outcropping with just enough room for Poe and BB-8. Beyond that, an inky blackness loomed. The hole in front of them looked deep and deadly, and Rey's exposed skin prickled with fear. If they'd rushed instead of taking their time, one of them could've fallen to their death.

Rose pressed her back into the wall of the tunnel and looked past Poe the same way Rey did, and her expression bore the same confusion Rey felt.

"It seems like there should be some sort of pathway here," Rose said, pointing to the soft green light emanating from an opening on the other side of the cavern.

"Maybe there's usually a drawbridge," Rey said. Rose was right. The emptiness separated them from the puddle of green light on the other side. And the food smell was stronger than it had been the entire trip, almost as though it was coming from the lighted path on the other side of the seemingly bottomless abyss.

BB-8 beeped again, something about humans and their lack of scanners, before rolling forward quickly. Poe yelled, and Rose cried out, her hand covering her mouth in fright.

But BB-8 just floated in the air, rolling back and forth and chirping an encouragement for everyone to follow him.

"Oh, it's . . . invisible," Rey said, using her staff to feel the walkway she couldn't see. The metal clanked sharply against a bridge of the same black rock as the tunnel.

Rose frowned and looked around the cavern. "It must be the way the lights from the plants are angled," she said. "The cavern looks bottomless, but it's really that the path is hidden."

"It's a brilliant defense," Poe said. "If we didn't have Beebee-Ate, we would've turned back and gone another way."

"I wonder who these potential allies are," Rey said, her gaze still on the emptiness a few centimeters in front of her toes. It was unnerving to stand on a path she couldn't see. Even her use of the Force hadn't prepared her for an invisible bridge. She still liked being able to see the things in front of her.

"I don't know, but if they're half as smart as they seem, they might be able to help us take down the First Order," Poe said.

Rey began to walk. Poe and Rose fell into step behind her, and they made their way slowly across the invisible path. Rey experimented to see how far the walkway went on her left and right, poking at the ground with her staff. She was dismayed to realize that the path was no wider than the length of her staff. A misstep could send any of them careening into the dark.

BB-8 waited in the entryway to the tunnel, his beeps excited as he urged them along. When everyone had crossed and entered the tunnel on the other side, Rey took a deep breath and let it out.

"Okay, less of that, maybe," she said.

"Definitely less of that," Poe said, still looking a little shaken.

"Are you here to provide assistance?" someone chirped.

Rey readied her staff, and both Rose and Poe drew their blasters. A small figure detached from the shadows and wobbled toward them. The figure reached Rey's shoulder, even though a good bit of that height was from the tall ears. Short, dense green fur covered its body, and it wore a smart tunic of deepest purple and a bandolier weighed down with explosives, blasters, and other weapons. Long, black claws protruded from the paws, and the dark eyes were large and inquisitive, shining in the near dark of the tunnel.

"You are Rey," the being said, pointing at Rey.

She nodded. "How did you know?"

"The leaves sing your name," the creature said, with an expression that looked almost like a smile but was really just a shifting of whiskers. "I am Lim. Are you hungry?"

They stood in a small antechamber, a guardhouse from the look of it. There were small, squat chairs of the same rock as the walls and a fire pit that warmed the room, chasing away the slight chill that stalked the tunnels. Suspended over the fire on a spit was a pot. In it bubbled the source of the delicious aroma they'd been smelling, and Rey's mouth watered as she looked at it.

"You made us . . . food?" she asked, still unsure whether Lim was offering.

"Yes! You are honored guests. You have come to help us defeat the First Order's soldiers before they destroy Minfar. The least I can do is feed you before you risk your lives to save us."

Rey looked back at Poe and Rose, but Poe was already sinking down on a seat and sniffing at the food appreciatively. "That smells delicious. What is it?"

"Blagaret soup," Lim said, hurrying over to ladle food into bowls with oddly spaced rings around the outside. Rey holstered her staff while Poe and Rose did the same with their blasters. As Rey watched she realized the rings on the cuplike dinnerware were for the claws on Lim's paws, and as Rey took the steaming dish of food, she had to spread her fingers to insert them in the rings. It was awkward, but she eventually figured it out. She sniffed the concoction deeply before trying it. The food was thick and hot, with a deliciously heady spice that prickled her taste buds and made her nose water just a little.

"It's spicy!" she cried.

"Here, have some juice." Lim handed Rey another dish, taller and narrower but still with the attached rings, and Rey drank it gratefully. The juice was sweet and tangy, and made the soup taste even better.

As Rey continued to eat she realized how hungry she was, and a quick glance at Rose and Poe reminded her how long it had been since they'd had a decent meal. The welcoming on Minfar was just what they needed. BB-8 rolled around and did a few tricks while they ate, and by the time they were done even Lim was making a snuffling sound Rey took for laughter. "Your droid is very funny," Lim said solemnly.

After they had drank and eaten their fill, Lim instructed them to drop their dishes into a shimmering pool nearby. They'd no sooner done that than Lim was heading toward a different tunnel than they'd initially come down, this one glowing in shades of blue. "Come, we have tarried long enough. Jem is expecting you." Lim took off down the tunnel, not bothering to look back to see if everyone followed.

Rey exchanged glances with Rose and Poe, shrugged, and then followed along, BB-8 beeping merrily as they headed deeper underground.

# CHAPTER 8

GLENNA KIP STOOD near the entry door to the transport and watched with pursed lips as the First Order flametroopers used their flame packs to burn down the jungle. The fire shot out, hot and orange, and the burning plants clogged the air with thick black smoke. In just a few short minutes they'd already cleared a sizable piece of land, and the resulting landscape was a scorched wound compared with the lush foliage beyond.

Glenna tried not to let the destruction bother her. She knew the choice she'd made when she answered the summons to work for the First Order. But this wanton devastation was something she hadn't bargained for. If she had her way, everyone would load back onto the transports and return to the *Ladara Vex* immediately.

But she was a scientist, not a First Order officer, so she was trapped watching the beautiful Minfarian jungle burn.

She'd been on Minfar for less than an hour, and she was already dismayed at the way the operation was unfolding. And not just the savage way the troopers were destroying the landscape. Branwayne—she called him that because she couldn't bear to think of the man as any kind of real officer; his affectations were just too ridiculous—had ordered a command post to be set up at this remote location, far from where Glenna had indicated she thought the labs might be located. This was not only a foolish endeavor but a waste of time.

They should be looking for the labs, not setting up a command post to wage war against a small group of Resistance fighters and their outdated ship.

Glenna smoothed her bodysuit—she'd prefer her usual drape dress, but a trip through the wilderness required a different approach—and went to find Branwayne. If she was stuck watching the First Order waste time trying to hunt down a handful of rebels, she was going to make sure she at least achieved her own personal goals.

Which had nothing to do with quashing the Resistance.

Glenna found Commander Spiftz in a command module tent, peering at the same three-dimensional hologram of Minfar she had showed him just hours earlier. As she entered the tent, Branwayne looked up and gave her a nod but didn't pause in his discussion with the infantry captains.

"This is the location where the *Falcon* went down, correct?" he said, looking to the same young analyst who'd told him about his lost TIE fighters earlier on the bridge. The girl looked impossibly young, her skin pale with a smattering of freckles across her nose. Glenna didn't know the girl's name, as few of the technicians within Branwayne's command lasted more than a few months, but the girl was calm as she adjusted Commander Spiftz's marker on the hologram.

"Here, sir. This is where the ship went down. And I don't know that it was the *Millennium Falcon*, sir. Just that it was a Corellian freighter."

"It was the *Falcon*," another analyst chimed in.

"We only know it was a Corellian model."

The two analysts were on the verge of a full-scale argument. The heat of Minfar must have been getting to them already for them to lose their military bearing so easily. Branwayne held up a gloved hand, forestalling any more bickering.

"Which happens to be the same model as the *Falcon*," Branwayne said with a dismissive wave. "We need to send out a patrol to sweep through the jungle right there, there, and there." He pointed to spots that surrounded the projected crash site. Glenna swallowed a sigh. Three teams sent out to search the jungle for the Resistance meant there would be no one left to search for the laboratories. Already most of the *Ladara Vex*'s landing party was engaged in establishing a command post and setting up communications relays. All for a mission that was only supposed to last a couple of days. Something must have changed. Glenna would find out just what that was and then make sure it didn't interfere with her own plans.

She waited patiently as Branwayne finished giving orders, his expression brimming with unchecked delight. This was no good. Commander Spiftz was usually a taciturn, sullen man, only bothering to talk when an order could be given. Whatever had put him in this joyous mood had to be something even bigger than finding the Resistance.

"Branwayne," Glenna said with a smile. She kept her expression pleasant, her voice low so the commander couldn't help turning to her.

"Is it everything you imagined?" he asked, gesturing to the burning jungle visible behind him.

"Is what?" Glenna asked, slightly disarmed by the turn of the conversation.

"Minfar! You've researched and studied it. And now you're finally here. This must feel like quite the accomplishment."

Glenna turned and looked in the direction Commander Spiftz pointed, just as a trooper pointed his flamethrower in the direction of a knot of trees. A host of small, cerulean flying creatures took to the air to avoid the weapon, and black smoke billowed up in their wake.

"Yes, it is rather something. I'm afraid I never could have imagined such a spectacle."

Commander Spiftz nodded, taking Glenna's words at face value. The man was an imbecile. That was the reason she'd sought him out in the first place. A petty, selfish officer, he cared about nothing but glory and the resultant promotions. Glenna had discussed the lost laboratories with half a dozen First Order officers in her bid to win support, and none of them had been half as simple as Branwayne. The man didn't crave wealth or friendship; he just wanted to be envied.

Which was perfect when Glenna's mission was to recover the Echo Horn before Hidreck could. She could use Branwayne's ambitions to her advantage.

Glenna had nearly cheered when she realized how silly the man's needs were. But that was before she had to compete with the possibility of the Resistance. Now she wished she'd tied her lot to one of the officers motivated purely by greed.

"Branwayne," Glenna said, pulling her attention back to the present. "I'm afraid I don't quite understand what is happening right now. When we left the cruiser I was under the impression it was in an effort to make a more concerted push to find the laboratories. But it looks as though chasing after that freighter has taken priority."

"The *Millennium Falcon* is the most coveted ship in all of the galaxy. It has a history going all the way back to the days of the Empire. It's a symbol of resistance and hope, and capturing it, as well as the rebels on board, would be a coup of unprecedented proportions. I have a mere two days until Commander Hidreck will be here, and I have been tasked with establishing a base of operations by then."

Glenna looked at the three flashing points of light surrounding the spot where it was thought the ship had gone down. "I take it you've decided to use that time to capture the *Millennium Falcon* and track down the rebels."

Commander Spiftz gave Glenna a smile that was downright patronizing, and if she'd been capable of anger she would have felt it in that moment. But in truth she could not feel anything beyond a sharp annoyance over the inconvenience. Glenna had been researching the very nature of the galaxy when Branwayne's grandparents had been babes in the womb, and his insolence was ill advised to say the least.

"That is very dismaying," Glenna said. "I'd hoped to be able to find the lab and the weapons cache there before we were interfered with by any . . . interlopers." She made sure to emphasize that last word so Branwayne would remember their plan. "But I suppose Commander Hidreck will be just as capable of transporting the cache back to the First Order."

Commander Spiftz straightened a little as he remembered that there were two goals, two opportunities for glory. His gaze landed on the hologram once more, going back to the spot Glenna had pointed out earlier in the day, and he sighed.

"For today, I believe it best if we focus on corralling the rebels. But tomorrow, perhaps we can send a small team out to investigate. I do understand your frustration, Madame Kip, but I must focus on this matter first and foremost."

Glenna inclined her head, not even bothering to correct his lack of proper address, and left the tent without another word. She could see a lost cause better than most, and although her goals remained the same, it appeared a new route was required.

Glenna made her way back to the transport. Commander Spiftz might be more focused on finding rebels on Minfar, but Glenna would not be thwarted.

She would find the lab, even if it meant going out into the jungle all by herself. She would find the legendary weapon before Hidreck arrived and claimed the prize for herself.

The Echo Horn would be Glenna's.

# CHAP

This tunr
up t

THEY WALKED for what seemed like hours. Lim, their furry green guide, led the way, with Rey, Poe, and Rose following behind.

Poe couldn't really tell one tunnel from another; the only thing that changed was the color of the plants lighting the way. He half supposed they were walking in circles, but something told him they weren't. Besides, BB-8 would know if Lim was trying to trick them or lead them into a trap and would give everyone plenty of warning.

At least, that's what Poe told himself.

They approached a shaft of sunlight and Lim stilled, waving for everyone's attention and pointing up at the hole. "That is where we fought the First Order last time.

el doubles back the way we came. We have to go
ere to get to the city. Be very quiet as we go."

Poe nodded, readying his blaster. Rose and Rey did
the same. Lim's whiskers twitched, and Poe wondered if
that signaled approval. The small green creature took a
strange-looking ball out of the bandolier instead of one of
the blasters, and Poe wondered what their guide was going
to do with it. Was that some kind of explosive?

Lim stopped and turned back toward them. "We will
have to walk through the jungle a small bit to get to the
other tunnel. The entrance is hidden, so you will have to
wait for me to open it." Lim waited until everyone nodded their understanding before continuing. Their guide
walked up the steep path to the surface, and Rey, Rose,
and Poe followed. At the top of the path Lim pushed some
of the dense foliage aside, and what had looked like a solid
wall of large fronds resolved into an opening. Poe couldn't
tell if the plant leaves had been woven together or if it
was another illusion like the bridge back in the cavern,
but either way, it was impressive. He never would've realized the plants blocked an opening, even from inside the
tunnel.

Once Lim cleared the way, they all exited and Poe had
to blink rapidly as his eyes adjusted to the bright sunlight. The heat and humidity hit him once more, and he

took a deep breath, already missing the cool air below. BB-8 whizzed by, unfazed by the change of terrain or temperature.

Lim indicated that they should crouch, and they began making their slow way to the entrance of the other tunnel, ducking below the large leafy fronds of the trees and plants of the jungle. Poe kept trying to sneak peeks of where they were going, but all he could see was a thick wall of leaves. A long myriapod with hundreds of legs fell from a plant onto Poe's arm. He knocked the bug away without a word, hiding his shiver of disgust.

As much as he liked traveling to new places, he was always a little cautious of the animals on new planets. You never knew what was safe and what would try to eat you.

Lim pointed them to another tunnel like the one they'd gone down the first time, a giant hole hidden under one of the leafy plants, but a crashing sound came through the trees. Everyone froze, blasters ready as the noise got closer.

"Approaching coordinates now. Will advise when on location."

The clacking of stormtrooper armor split the serenity of the jungle while the echoing squawk of the radio sent a trio of flying creatures into the air. Poe peered up over the foliage to get a good view of the First Order soldiers walking right toward them. There were six in all, and there was no way the rebels could run to the tunnel and disappear before they were seen.

They were going to have to fight.

"On the count of three," Poe said. But he didn't even get a chance to count. Lim stood up, chirruped something loud and terrifying, and threw the ball thing at the approaching stormtroopers.

The ball, which Poe could see also had a string attached, hit one, then another, then a third stormtrooper, knocking them senseless so they fell to the ground, dropping their weapons as they went. Lim then yanked the orb back, winding the string up for another attack. The remaining three stormtroopers tried to return fire, but Rose, Rey, and Poe were much faster. Their aims were true, each of them stunning one of the remaining stormtroopers.

"Wow," Poe said to Lim. "That was amazing."

"I know," Lim said, this time the twitch of whiskers seeming pleased. "We have to get going before they wake up."

Lim ran toward the tunnel, and Rey and Rose followed, Poe bringing up the rear. BB-8 rolled past him, moving at full speed. Poe was almost to the tunnel when a stormtrooper called, "Halt! Poe Dameron, halt!"

Poe turned and fired blindly, not bothering to aim properly. Another group of stormtroopers ran up, firing their weapons, and Poe decided it was a good time to retreat. He dove down the tunnel just as a blaster bolt slammed into a nearby tree.

As Poe slid down the tunnel, the sound of the injured tree falling echoed behind him. Sand and pebbles rained down on him as his boots hit the bottom of the tunnel slide. Rey and Rose were waiting for him with worried expressions.

"Thank goodness you're okay!" Rose said, her lips pressed together with concern.

"Yeah, I'm fine. I was spotted by stormtroopers, though. And they recognized me!"

"Oh, that's bad," Rey said.

"I mean, maybe," Poe said, grinning from ear to ear. "The First Order knows who I am!"

BB-8 let out an annoyed beep, and Rose frowned. "But now the First Order knows we're here for sure."

Some of Poe's excitement drained away, but not all. The First Order was huge, and the fact that they knew who he was—Poe Dameron—well . . .

It was pretty amazing. He was famous!

Rey's expression turned grim, and she glanced back up the tunnel. "What happened with the entrance?"

"One of the stormtroopers hit a tree, and it fell over and covered the hole. I don't think they saw me go down

the tunnel. But even if they did and they try to follow us, it should take them a while to clear the way."

"We must hurry then," Lim said. "We still have far to go, and if the stormtroopers get into the tunnels we will need to be ready."

Poe nodded, and their little group set out once more.

Hopefully, they'd make it to the city without any other mishaps.

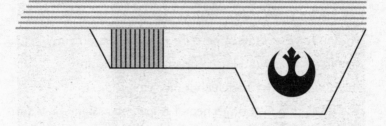

# CHAPTER 10

COMMANDER BRANWAYNE SPIFTZ was enjoying a nutritious dinner of sala leaf stew when a very flustered-looking lieutenant burst into his tent. The man struggled for breath, and Commander Spiftz calmly set down his spoon and wiped his mouth.

"Aderat," Spiftz said, recognizing the recently disgraced lieutenant. His uniform looked marginally better than the last time Spiftz had seen him, but it was still not quite up to *Ladara Vex* standards. How frustrating. "Is there a reason you've interrupted my evening meal?"

"My apologies, sir. But we got the ship. The Corellian light freighter."

The commander put down his bowl and gave Aderat his full attention. "And?"

Aderat gave a short nod. "It's the *Millennium Falcon*."

Satisfaction surged through Spiftz, and the barest hint of a smile flitted around his mouth. He wasn't the type to celebrate—it was unbecoming in a First Order officer—but gloating was well within decorum. Now everyone would see what kind of hero he was. He could nearly hear the cheers that would accompany his promotion.

*Admiral* Spiftz had such a nice ring to it.

"Well, that is good to hear. I hope you assigned a team to guard it for when the rebels inevitably return," Spiftz said, giving Aderat a tight-lipped smile.

"Yes, sir. But there's more." Aderat struggled for his next words, his face flushing as he chose them carefully.

Commander Spiftz waited as the man coughed once more and then composed himself. "Commander Spiftz. The Resistance has been located. Our stormtroopers engaged them a short time ago."

If his stormtroopers had already captured the rebel scum, then he was ahead of schedule. By the time Commander Hidreck reached Minfar, he'd be on his way back to the Outer Rim and the nearest First Order stronghold, the Resistance and a legendary weapon both firmly in his control.

Coming to this detestable planet had definitely been the right course of action. Things were almost going too well.

"Excellent," Commander Spiftz said, standing and placing his napkin on the table. "Bring them to me immediately so I can interrogate them."

Aderat blinked once, twice, and then had the gall to frown. "Who did you want me to bring to you?"

Commander Spiftz swallowed his frustration. The man was an annoyance and obtuse besides. "The rebels, of course."

"Oh, my apologies, sir, but the Resistance agents weren't captured. They got away, in the same manner the local fighters have."

"And what manner is that, Aderat?" Commander Spiftz's good mood evaporated, leaving him even more annoyed than he had been before.

"Well, sir, they disappeared."

"'They disappeared.'" Commander Spiftz lowered his voice, struggling to contain his rage. Aderat continued to be a disappointment. Incompetent to the end. If they'd been on a larger ship, Spiftz would have sent the man to be reassigned as a stormtrooper. But he couldn't afford the loss of an officer.

"Send the stormtrooper who made the report to speak to me."

Relief was etched in Aderat's features, and the man snapped a crisp salute before leaving the tent. Commander

Spiftz paced while he waited. From what Aderat had reported, two things were certain: the Resistance was definitely on Minfar, and they were working with the local populace, who had been frustrating the search for the legendary weapon for weeks.

There was nothing remarkable or strategic about Minfar. The planet was too far away from anything of merit to make sense as a rebel base or even as a logistics center. The logical conclusion was that the Resistance was on the planet searching for the Echo Horn, the same as Commander Spiftz.

The stormtrooper entered the tent, her heavy armor clanking loudly as she moved. At first there was nothing remarkable about the soldier; she looked just like every other white-armored trooper on the *Ladara Vex*. But upon closer inspection, Commander Spiftz noted the blackened spot in the center of the stormtrooper's chest.

Someone had shot her with a blaster. Set for stun, apparently.

"You encountered the Resistance while on a patrol," Commander Spiftz said, sitting back down in his chair and continuing his evening meal.

"Yes, sir. We were engaged by the Resistance and a local fighter after crossing check point number two."

Commander Spiftz brought up the hologram of Minfar

once more. "What were the coordinates of the skirmish?"

As the stormtrooper gave the coordinates, a new spot of color bloomed on the hologram. This one was blue. It was quite some distance from where they'd supposed the *Millennium Falcon* had gone down.

But it was close to a spot Glenna Kip had marked as a possible location for the lost laboratories.

"Did you recognize any of the Resistance fighters that engaged you?"

"Yes, sir. Poe Dameron was among the group. He disappeared under some brush, but when we searched the area, all we found was debris."

"How do you know it was Poe Dameron?" Spiftz asked.

The stormtrooper shifted slightly. "Who else has that hair?"

Commander Spiftz gripped his spoon so hard that the metal bent. "Were you not told that the creatures of this planet, the Zixon, live underground? Perhaps they have entrances they have been using."

The stormtrooper said nothing, clearly at a loss for words, and Spiftz realized he would have to speak to Lieutenant Nivers about this. There was no reason a handful of Resistance fighters should be able to thwart a detachment of First Order soldiers so easily.

Not to mention that Poe Dameron, Resistance hero

and X-wing pilot extraordinaire, was on Minfar. Now Spiftz knew for certain that the Resistance was there to find the legendary weapon. There was no way General Organa would send Dameron to such a remote location unless there was something important to be gleaned from it.

"That is all. You are dismissed," Commander Spiftz said, and the stormtrooper saluted and left. Commander Spiftz went back to his soup, his mind turning over this new development as he ate.

By the time he finished his meal, he'd made up his mind. He wiped his mouth and dropped the napkin on the table. He needed to speak with Glenna Kip.

She would be delighted to know that their goals were no longer as divergent as they'd appeared earlier in the day. They had to find the legendary Echo Horn before the Resistance did.

Once the weapon was his, Commander Branwayne Spiftz would lay an epic trap for the Resistance. He would capture Poe Dameron and take possession of the *Millennium Falcon*. He would be a hero of the First Order. After that, anything he desired would be his for the taking.

It was a foolproof plan.

And nothing would stop him.

# CHAPTER 11

ROSE FOLLOWED Rey, Poe, and their furry green guide, Lim, in disbelief. It had been quite a day. First she'd fought against TIE fighters, then she'd gotten to explore an underground network of tunnels, and then there had been a whole firefight with stormtroopers. And that didn't even count meeting the fascinating Lim.

She never thought when she first started working with the Resistance that it would be so, well, exciting! It was so much more than just fixing things.

As they walked, she still couldn't help gawking at Lim and their surroundings. She was agog, not at meeting such a strange little being—she'd met lots of different kinds of people in her travels throughout the galaxy—but at the construction and engineering involved in building such a complex tunnel structure.

Rose liked to know how things worked. It was what made her such a great mechanic. So as they'd walked along the tunnels, she'd marveled at how anyone or anything could build such a massive underground structure, seemingly without tools. She hadn't seen any terrain movers or the telltale tracks they left on the ground. The walls were so smooth and perfect, they looked like they'd occurred naturally in the shiny black rock. But the plants that lit the way had a more purposeful feel to them, as though someone had put them there for that reason. It was a mystery, and while Rose didn't usually mind mysteries, she minded this one.

Because the tunnels made her nervous.

Rose couldn't quite explain the feeling, but it had been there ever since they'd crossed the invisible bridge: the sensation of being watched, of something following and biding its time. After they'd slid into the new tunnel, she'd thought it might be stormtroopers, but the First Order would've attacked by then if it was them. This was something else, something or someone sneaky.

She looked over her shoulder frequently, checking for the barest hint of someone walking behind them.

But every time she looked, there was nothing but shadows.

BB-8 stopped and moved toward Rose, letting out a mournful beep.

"You can feel it, too, Beebee?" Rose said, her voice low. She didn't want the others to hear her. After all, she wasn't like Rey or Poe. Rey had the Force, and Poe had been a military hero long before Rose and her sister joined the Resistance. Rose was just Rose, and right then she felt like a little kid afraid of her own shadow.

BB-8 beeped an affirmative to her question, and Rose felt validated. "Do you know what it is? Or who?" Rose asked, and BB-8's response was clearly a negative.

"Well, at least you sense it, too," Rose said, feeling a little bit better.

Even if they were being tracked by something.

They walked for a short while longer, a different kind of light filtering in. While the tunnel they'd walked through had been cast in deep blue, the light ahead was a bright yellow, like that of a sunny day. Their guide picked up the pace, fairly skipping along before them. Rose hurried to keep up, the light up ahead seeming infinitely more welcoming than whatever lurked in the ambient glow behind them.

The noise of the city greeted them before the sight of it did. The tunnel narrowed suddenly, and Rose was forced to crouch to get through the opening to the space beyond. Up ahead, Rey and Poe had stopped on a ledge that overlooked the city, and Rose could see why.

It was like nothing she'd ever seen before.

Below them stretched a magnificent city and country-side. An abundance of sunshine streamed into the space somehow, painting everything with a warm glow. Houses were clustered together in seemingly random configurations, octagonal shapes pressed against and on top of one another in a beautiful sculpture. The houses looked small to Rose, like something built for children. Green trailing vines draped off of balconies and hung over lintels, and a riotous assortment of flowers bloomed here and there on the vines. There were a number of the small green creatures talking and walking and doing the usual living of people everywhere.

Beyond the clusters of houses were verdant green fields with rows of evenly spaced plants. Figures moved between the rows, tending the plants. It looked as though the denizens of the planet lived and worked all within that single space.

For a moment Rose thought they'd somehow gone back above the surface, but when she looked up she realized that the space was underground. The walls arched upward, disappearing into whatever cast the daylight from above. Once more, Rose wondered how these small beings had created such an amazing place. It would have been a lot of work.

STAR WARS

Their guide continued down a slope, and Rey, Poe, and Rose followed. BB-8 ranged ahead, as though he suddenly knew where they were going. Rose frowned.

"Where is Beebee-Ate headed?" she asked Poe and Rey.

Rey shrugged, but Poe grinned. "If I know that droid, he's been tracking the signal from the broadcast since we got here. It's probably how he knew which way to go back in the jungle."

"Ah, that was a good idea," Rose said. The little droid was sort of like the people of Minfar: small but very resourceful. No one should underestimate either of them.

Rose just hoped someone would be able to help her find the parts she needed to fix the *Millennium Falcon*.

They continued down the path, which was made of the same black rock as the tunnels. The houses, though, looked to be made of some kind of mud, and as they walked, the houses shaded from yellow to purple to orange and then back to black, as though the builders had used various kinds of mud to create them. When combined with the flowering vines, the effect was breathtaking. The scent of the flowers filled the air, clearing away the slightly musty smell that plagued the tunnels.

That place was one of the most amazing things Rose had ever seen, and when Rey and Poe came to a halt, Rose was so busy gawking that she walked right into Poe's back.

"Oh, sorry," she said.

"It's really something, huh?" Poe said, gesturing to the buildings around them.

"Yes! The plants and the tunnels, and what do you think made the walls so smooth? Do you think it was our friend and their people? And how good was that meal?" At Poe's wide-eyed expression, Rose laughed. "Sorry, I'm kind of nervous and excited. Have you ever seen anything like this before?"

Poe shook his head. "No, definitely never underground. You're right, this place is incredible."

"It took the elders a hundred years to build Ghikjil," someone said.

Rose tore her gaze away from the architecture and turned toward a person standing next to their guide. Like Lim, this being also wore a purple tunic, but a shiny star-shaped plant smaller than Rose's palm dangled from the newcomer's neck. Their guide seemed to defer to this other person, and Rose wondered if it was the mysterious Jem.

"You are the Resistance," the being said without any hesitation.

"Yes," Poe said while Rose and Rey nodded.

"You called us for help. We got your transmission," Rose said. "I'm Rose Tico."

"Poe Dameron," the pilot said, smiling widely.

"And I'm Rey. Uh, just Rey." She placed her staff back in its holster, and Rose took that as a signal to put her blaster away. It wouldn't do them any good to look hostile to their new friends.

"Very nice to meet you, Rose, Poe, and Rey. Oh, and Beebee-Ate, as well." The green-furred person addressed the astromech droid as he beeped a greeting. "I am Jem, the leader of the Zixon, which is the name of our people. This is Lim. She was sent out to greet you."

The Zixon who had led them through the tunnels inclined her head. Jem cleared his throat. "I am glad you were able to make it past the grobel unharmed."

"Grobel?" Poe asked.

"A massive beast that devours everything in its path. It is supposed by our scholars that once upon a time the grobel ruled these underground passages, but then the Zixon came to this place and made it something different. There have been fewer and fewer grobel of late, which means there are more and more Zixon."

"Do the grobel . . . eat you?" Rey asked.

Jem's whiskers twitched, which Rose took to be a sort of smile. "Only if they can catch us. They stalk the tunnels but will only attack if they think they have a clear advantage. We have many tricks to keep them away."

"This explains the cavern with the invisible bridge," Poe said.

Jem nodded. "Yes. The Zixon's enemies are numerous, but we are very good at defending ourselves. Come, follow me and we shall discuss the reason I sent for help."

Rose followed the rest of the group, sparing one final glance at the tunnels they'd come from. At least now she knew why she'd felt like she was being watched.

Because she was.

# CHAPTER 12

REY TRIED NOT TO STARE at the Zixon as she followed Jem, but the residents of Ghikjil seemed just as interested in her as she was in them. From their curious ears to their beautiful homes, Rey couldn't help feeling a connection to the peaceful creatures. She supposed it had something to do with the Force. Lim's strange comment when they met about how the leaves whispered her name pricked at Rey, so she made a note to ask Lim about it when they were alone. With all her frustration in the Force, it might be nice to talk to someone else about the connections of the galaxy, someone who maybe didn't know anything about the legends of the Jedi. How did the Zixon feel the Force? Did they know something about connecting with it that she didn't?

But Rey was certain that the sense of peace and harmony she felt inside the Zixon city wasn't just the Force making itself known. The place really was serene. Minfar was far from the First Order and the fallen New Republic, away from all the woe that followed wherever the First Order turned its attention.

At least it had been.

Rey tried to imagine the First Order storming Ghikjil, knocking down the houses and taking the Zixon away to a work camp. Or worse, designing weapons on Minfar and testing them on the local population, as they had on Rose's planet. Rey's fists clenched and her jaw tightened. Not if she could help it.

"Are you okay?" Rose whispered, and Rey relaxed her hands and gave Rose a wan smile.

"Yes, sorry, I was just thinking about the First Order coming here and . . ." Rey's voice trailed off, but understanding lit Rose's face.

"Don't worry, we aren't going to let that happen. As soon as we know what's going on we can send for help. I'm sure General Organa will send assistance."

Rey nodded, but she wasn't so sure. Not because she thought General Organa didn't care but because she didn't know how much help the Resistance could send. So far, thanks to a lot of work and a little luck, they had a small fleet of Mon Calamari and Corellian ships, and droids to help with operations. But there were not nearly enough Resistance fighters to take on any kind of significant First Order threat. And the First Order was a danger everywhere, not just on Minfar. Rey didn't know if perhaps other operations were happening, and if they were, how far away they were. What if there wasn't any help to offer?

The group walked a little farther, the houses getting a bit larger, until they came to a place that seemed to be a gathering hall. As they'd walked Zixon had been following along, coming out of their houses and leaving their work to join the procession. They murmured back and forth in a language that wasn't Basic, a series of whistles and chirps that were soothing rather than menacing. They could be talking about their visitors, but they seemed more curious than anything else.

A few Zixon were already in the gathering hall, and like Lim they were heavily armed. Their bandoliers held numerous blasters, all of them much older models. Rey wondered if the Zixon even used the blasters, since Lim seemed to prefer her ball-and-string weapon instead. The blasters didn't look very well cared for, and it would be difficult for the Zixon to use the trigger mechanisms with their large claws. It seemed like the blasters were more for decoration, and Lim was wearing more than any of the other Zixon with bandoliers.

Jem led Rey, Rose, and Poe to seats in the front row of a circle of small stones, all made of that strange, shiny black rock they'd seen in the tunnels. There was a fire pit in the middle, like the one at the guardhouse where they'd met Lim. In the pit, rather than a cook fire, was a communications module.

"This equipment doesn't seem to match the rest of their city," Rose murmured, and Rey agreed. How had the Zixon come by all these bits of technologically advanced tools?

"This is where we called out for assistance," Jem said. "This unit was given to us by a friend, who said to use it should there ever be trouble here on Minfar, especially should the stormtroopers return. They showed us the channel and programmed it for us. And here you are. Thank you for answering the call."

"Who is this friend of yours? Do they have a name?" Poe asked.

Jem's whiskers did another smile twitch. "We only know them as our friend."

"Wait, so this was given to you by your friend. You don't have any other stuff like this?" Rose asked.

"The Forbidden Lands have plenty of technology," Lim

said. "But we forbid all from going there. It is a place of much sorrow."

Poe frowned, and BB-8 beeped mournfully. "Maybe you could explain what you mean?" Poe said.

Jem nodded. "Long ago, just as now, a group of others came to Minfar. They taught us Basic and gave us gifts." He pointed to the blasters worn by Lim and the others dressed like her. Rey guessed they were the Zixon army. "But the gifts were just a ploy to distract us."

"They built a weapon and they tested it on us," Lim said, her voice low. "When it was turned on, we were hopelessly pulled to their land and unable to do anything but obey."

"A mind-control device?" Rey wondered aloud.

Jem's whiskers twitched in agitation. "No, our minds were our own. We were powerless to leave their land, however. And the people controlling us were not afraid to hurt us if we resisted their commands. It was more like we'd heard a song, a delightful song that we could not resist, even though we tried. It was like sleeping while awake."

"I tried fighting it," Lim said. "But the more I fought the more I began to . . . lose myself. And so I, we all, learned to listen and wait instead."

There was a subtle shift in the gathered crowd as the Zixon remembered those terrible days, and Rey was even more certain that they had to help the Zixon, no matter what. She couldn't let such an awful thing happen again.

"That's horrible," Rose said. Rey thought she was probably remembering the terrible things that had forced her and her sister to leave their own home on Hays Minor.

"How did you get free?" Poe asked.

Jem's whiskers twitched once more, this time in a glad way. "Our friend liberated us by stopping the machine, and then they taught us how to use the communication unit to call for assistance should the others return."

"But the machine is still there?" Poe asked. At Jem's nod, he crossed his arms. "That's why the First Order is here. They're probably looking for the weapon the Empire built."

"We have to stop them," Rose said, standing. "And we have to find a compressor housing to fix our ship before we can fight. We're better with a ship. At least we have better odds of winning."

"We do not use ships," Jem said. "So I do not think we can help you."

"But there are many things that might be useful in the Forbidden Lands," Lim said, her ears going flat. "We could lead an expedition there for you to look." It was clear that was the last thing she wanted to do. Lim was incredibly brave, and Rey thought that even if they hadn't been certain about whether or not to fight, that would have decided it. It was hard to help other people when you were scared, but Lim and the rest of the Zixon seemed like good, brave people.

Besides, they'd asked for the help of the Resistance, and Rey felt like that meant more than anything. The Zixon were about to be in a battle not just for their world but for their very lives. The Resistance would be nothing if it didn't stand up for people like that.

Rey nodded. "Okay, so it looks like we have a plan. First, repair the *Falcon*. And after that, find a way to get the First Order off of Minfar."

Poe grinned. "All in a day's work for the Resistance, huh?" he said, and Rey couldn't help but return his grin.

Once more, she understood why Poe enjoyed fighting the First Order.

Because if the Resistance didn't stop them, who would?

Jem's whiskers twisted into a grin. The expressions the Zixon's green-furred faces made were uncannily akin to human ones. Rey found herself smiling back at Jem. "Excellent. Thank you for coming to our aid, brave fighters of the Resistance. But for now, we shall welcome you in the proper style of the Zixon."

A line of dancers appeared out of nowhere, and music—a combination of squeaky horns and deep-voiced drums—kicked up a lively beat. Rose's face lit up as she jumped to her feet and began to clap in time to the music. Poe grinned wide, his cheeks flushing as one of the Zixon gave him a crown of flowers to wear.

"I, uh—thanks?" he said.

Rey and Rose were given crowns, as well, the flowers the same beautiful deep purple as Poe's. Rey sniffed the flower crown when no one was looking. She didn't want to appear rude, but she found it sweetly scented and utterly delightful. Even BB-8 got one, and he beeped his thanks to a shy Zixon who ran off with a chorus of squeaks and chitters.

Bowls of food were brought out, and Rey's stomach grumbled once more. If the food was even half as good as the stew they'd eaten in the tunnels, they were in for a treat.

The line of dancers began to wind through the gathering area, and as they went, one of the dancers invited Rose to join. Laughing, she trailed behind, trying to follow the steps but looking just a little lost. Lim and a group of Zixon who were dressed similarly sat next to Poe, and Lim translated as the Zixon, who were apparently warriors, asked Poe about his adventures with the Resistance. BB-8 rolled around some smaller Zixon, and they laughed and chased him as though he was a toy.

"Rey, this is okay?" Jem asked, coming to sit next to her.

"Oh, yes, this is delightful. Thank you."

"Thank you for coming. We hope you can help," Jem said with a solemn nod before he was called over to a group of Zixon to discuss something in a series of agitated whirs and chitters.

Rey smiled, feeling at ease and at peace. Even though she was happy to be having fun with the Zixon, she just hoped they could find a compressor housing the next day.

Because she could not let the First Order ruin all this.

# CHAPTER 13

GLENNA KIP WALKED behind the team of stormtroopers sullenly, watching and listening but not speaking. Her plan after talking to Commander Spiftz had been to slip out and find the Echo Horn by herself, but Lieutenant Nivers was entirely too good at keeping track of the comings and goings in her perimeter. Glenna had been only a few steps past the first set of defenses before Nivers appeared, demanding to know what Glenna was up to.

Nothing good for the First Order, of course. But she could hardly tell the young officer that.

So Glenna had changed tactics. Convincing Lieutenant Nivers to accompany her on the mission before night fell had been easier than she'd thought. It seemed that the newly appointed leader of the ground forces was just a tad bit desperate for some guidance and direction, two things Professor Glenna Kip was well equipped to provide.

"Are you certain that we're in the correct area?" Lieutenant Nivers asked as they passed through what looked to be an incredibly familiar bit of jungle.

"Not at all," Glenna said with a slight smile. "As I said, my research showed that the entrance to the labs was somewhere in this area. We are looking for anything that would indicate a large creature has been here, dirt scraped away with large claws or the like."

"I don't like this," Nivers said, her blaster at the ready.

"Minfar is home to many dangers, but being able to bring Commander Spiftz the Echo Horn will be well worth the risk, I assure you," Glenna said.

Nivers nodded and continued walking, oblivious to Glenna falling back just a bit. She wasn't leading the group to the entrance to the labs. She was steering them right toward a grobel's nest. Grobel were large, hungry, and not very picky creatures. They would enjoy a few stormtroopers as a snack.

While Nivers and her stormtroopers were occupied with the grobel, Glenna would proceed to the true entrance to the lost laboratories and secure the Echo Horn for herself. And once that was complete, she'd find a way to get as far away from Minfar and the First Order as possible.

But first she had to deal with the more immediate matter at hand: a squad of stormtroopers and a First Order lieutenant who was in way over her head.

The group continued their trek through the jungle. Nivers's face was flushed and sweaty, evidence of both the heat of the jungle and the difficulty of the terrain. The trees and underbrush pushed close together, making walking difficult. The air carried the dank, musky scent of soil and plant matter. It was a wholly nice place to be in Glenna's opinion, even though she couldn't reveal to anyone in the First Order just how many times she'd been to Minfar.

Even though she'd told Branwayne that all her data were based on research, that was a lie. Minfar was like a second home to Glenna.

The distance between trees began to widen a bit, and just as Glenna's feet sank into a bit of freshly churned dirt, a shout went up from the stormtroopers at the front of the column. An answering roar made Glenna slow her pace and then take a step back.

They had found the grobel's nest.

Although Glenna's view of the grobel was partially obscured by the trees and surrounding vegetation, she knew what the stormtroopers had found: a large beast, nearly the size of a transport ship, covered in brilliant rainbow gemstones hard enough to protect its soft underbelly and grind tunnels through the planet. Once the grobel had ruled the underground of Minfar, but that was before the Zixon learned to fight. Before Glenna taught them how they could repel the grobel from the tunnels and live full and happy lives.

But Glenna did not have time to think about her friends. She got the opportunity she had been waiting for as the grobel, with its cavernous mouth lined with rows of sharp teeth, turned around and gobbled up a stormtrooper nearly whole.

The rest of the stormtroopers, five of them plus Lieutenant Nivers, began firing their blasters at the ravenous beast that had just eaten their colleague. Glenna could have told them that their blasters wouldn't work against the massive creature, as the gemstones studding its sides had a curious way of deflecting the bolts in every direction, leaving the grobel unharmed but agitated. Glenna stepped backward and melted into the shadows.

It wasn't far to the entrance to the labs, and Glenna Kip was fast, faster than a human. She sprinted through the trees, dodging low-hanging branches and an occasional web to stop in front of a mountainside that jutted out of the ground, the black rock a stark contrast to the red dirt below.

The secret entrance to the laboratories. She was so close to accomplishing her mission. The door to the labs was part of the mountainside, but up close one could see where door and stone met. Glenna and her original research team had worked for weeks to make the entrance look like part of the natural landscape, using giant machines to mine the local rock. It was why the labs were so hard to find. There was nothing unusual about the mountain on a scan of the planet's surface; every single trace of technology was muted under the strange properties of Minfar's deep minerals.

Glenna walked to the sleek edge of the rock, just as she had so many times in the past. This time, though, would be different. This time she would destroy all the terrible inventions inside, because she had made a promise.

"Professor Kip!"

Glenna's hand stilled a short distance from the keypad to the lab. She turned as Lieutenant Nivers and a single stormtrooper stumbled into the clearing.

"Professor Kip, we have to get back to the base. That creature—it—it ate almost my entire squad!" There was no way to see the expression of the lone remaining storm-trooper, but Glenna was willing to bet it was somewhere between horror and shock.

Everyone panicked a little the first time they met a grobel.

Glenna nodded and walked toward Nivers, hoping the officer wouldn't notice the the black mountain behind Glenna. But Nivers looked past Glenna, her eyes widening as she spotted the doorway over her shoulder.

"Those are the labs!" Nivers said. "I did it! I found it!"

Glenna opened her mouth to make some excuse but quickly snapped it shut. She knew when a plan had stopped being effective, and there would be no way to convince the lieutenant that the wall of mountain behind them was nothing more than part of the natural landscape. Glenna was no Jedi who could use the Force to sway the woman's mind.

"Yes, indeed, I do believe that is the case. We should return to the base and let Commander Spiftz know." Glenna paused as though she was considering. "Unless, of course, you think it would be better to make certain first. Perhaps by getting another team to open the lab?"

Nivers nodded, frowning as she thought. "Perhaps. I wouldn't want to tell the commander I'd found the labs without making sure."

"Of course not. Especially after losing those stormtroopers. You do know how Commander Spiftz is about resources." Glenna added a reassuring smile to the last bit.

Nivers shook off her hesitancy and straightened. "Yes, that is a much better idea. Commander Spiftz would be sorely vexed to know that I'd lost stormtroopers and had nothing to show for it. Thank you, Professor Kip, your help has been appreciated, but I think we can take it from here. You should return to camp. I believe you know the way?"

Glenna nodded and swallowed a sigh as Nivers directed the stormtrooper to mark down the coordinates to the lab and request reinforcements to open the doors. She turned and walked into the woods, returning to camp as she'd been directed.

She'd been so close to finding the Echo Horn and destroying it. But she couldn't give up just yet. Keeping Nivers from relaying the information would buy her some additional time to figure out her next steps. Whatever she did, she would have to make sure she got to the Echo Horn before Branwayne Spiftz did.

As she walked through the dark, surefooted and swift, Glenna Kip began to think. She would find another way to stop the First Order from finding the devastating weapon. After all, Minfar was a planet of many surprises.

# CHAPTER 14

POE SMOTHERED A YAWN and followed Jem as he made his way through Ghikjil. A little way off, Rose and Rey murmured, exclaiming over the creek that wound through the town, brightly colored fish visible in the dark water. Gentle fluttering creatures had come out to sup on the flowering vines, which had begun to glow softly. Overhead, the sun was starting to dim, signaling the rest period for the Zixon. Rose had spent quite a few moments during the party asking their hosts everything there was to know about Ghikjil, most especially about the seemingly artificial sun. The light was created by a series of mirrors set into a large overhead tube. The mirrors reflected the Minfarian sunlight down into the cavern so the plants could grow, but they were impossible to find from the surface.

"Our sun tube is located in a very dangerous part of Minfar, in the middle of a treacherous mountain range. If we were to go straight up, it would be very high, with lots of dangerous enemies," Jem had explained while Rose listened, eyes wide with wonder.

But that had been a while ago, and Poe needed sleep. It had been a very long day, and the next promised to be even more eventful. Jem and Lim had promised to take them to the Forbidden Lands, and once they'd fixed the *Falcon*, they'd have to figure out just how many First Order soldiers there were on Minfar. Poe might like giving the First Order what for, but he also knew better than to run into a situation without knowing the odds.

Before, he would've demanded that they find the labs in the dark, repair the *Falcon*, and take the First Order by surprise. It would be impulsive and risky, and later he'd wonder if it had been a good idea. But after everything that had happened and all the friends he'd lost, including Rose's sister, Poe was more cautious. Victory wasn't worth lives, and with so few allies left, he had to be smarter about taking risks.

And no matter what their chances of success looked like, a good night's rest was key.

Jem stopped in front of a house built to human specifications rather than the much smaller ones of the Zixon. The windows were twice as large as any of the other houses, and the door loomed above Jem.

"When our friend came to visit, they would stay here, but it has been a long while since they have graced us with their presence. You can rest in this place. I will have someone send you breakfast early tomorrow, and then we will begin our travels to the Forbidden Lands." When Jem said it that way, it sounded fearsome. Poe wondered just what about the location was so terrifying to the Zixon.

He supposed they would find out soon.

"Hey, Jem," Poe said, something occurring to him. "Are you sure you don't have a name for this person, this friend you keep speaking of?" Something about the whole mystery friend situation bothered Poe, like an itch in the middle of his back that he couldn't quite reach. "They obviously cared about your people very much, and helped you out of a really bad situation."

"Our friend never gave us their name. They said names gave people power over each other. But they helped us settle this place, and showed us how to build the sun tube. Before that, my kind were hunted by the much larger creatures aboveground. We hid amongst the trees, and there were never more than thirty or forty of our kind at any given time. Those were very bad days. Our friend showed us how to make useful weapons, how to survive down here, safely." Jem's whiskers twitched. "They even showed us how to keep the grobel away without getting hurt ourselves. We owe much to our friend. Now, you must rest. I will see you in the morning."

"Good night," Rose and Rey called as Jem left, making his way back down the path they'd just traveled.

"Anyone else wondering who this friend of theirs was?" Poe asked.

Rey frowned. "Not especially, but they do seem like a very generous person. Why, do you think it was someone we know?"

"Maybe?" Poe said, opening the door to the house. "Jem and Lim mentioned their friend a couple of times, and I was just wondering, well, what if it was Skywalker?"

"Luke Skywalker?" Rose breathed, and Poe could almost see her eyes turn to hearts at the prospect.

"Yeah," Poe said, entering the house. The place was cozy and warm, even as the temperature outside the house dropped. The only furnishings were several purple shapes in varying sizes. Were those supposed to be beds and chairs? Not that Poe was complaining; he had slept in much worse places. Even if it had been a room full of rocks he would've made do. "He was missing for a long while. What if he was the one who came here and liberated the Zixon?"

Rey frowned. "I don't know. I met Luke. He didn't exactly seem like the kind of guy who would hang out and wear flower crowns."

Poe yawned. "They said the weapon used on them was designed by the Empire. Luke Skywalker helped defeat the Empire."

"We don't know that he *wasn't* here," Rose said, running her hand across the fuzzy fabric of a chair. "Maybe even for a little bit. What if the Force led him here long ago, and led us here now to help the Zixon? What if we're meant to be here, and not just because we got the distress call?"

Poe sank into a fluffy chair and kicked his feet out, sighing. It felt nice to have a moment just to relax, to spend some time considering all that had happened in the past day. He'd started the day loading supplies and ended it meeting the Zixon. And in between had been a nice moment of blasting TIE fighters and stormtroopers. He had to say, it was a pretty good day.

But Rey was nowhere near as relaxed. She scowled as she dropped her staff next to the door, her pack falling beside it, and carefully removed the holster that held her blaster. "If I was better at this whole Force thing then I'd probably have an answer."

"I don't know, maybe," Rose said, dropping into a chair similar to the one Poe lounged in. She leaned back against the strange purple material. "But maybe you're doing exactly what the Force wants you to. Isn't that how the Force works? Everything happens for a reason, even if that reason isn't clear until after everything has calmed down. Oh, this is really comfy." Rose sighed. "Way more comfortable than the *Falcon*."

BB-8 beeped his disagreement, and Poe shrugged. "No charging port, you're right. Sorry about that, buddy. Are you going to be okay until we get back to the *Falcon*?"

BB-8 beeped an affirmative and rolled off.

"Can we go back to this weapon Jem was talking about?" Rey asked, beginning to pace. "Do you think that's what brought the First Order here?"

"Maybe," Rose said, considering her words. She pursed her lips in contemplation. "Maybe we should try to find this weapon before the First Order does."

Poe sat up. "Wait, you think we should take and use the weapon that enslaved the Zixon?"

"No! I mean, not to enslave anyone," Rose said, flushing. Rey stopped pacing, and Rose continued her explanation. "But maybe there are other uses for it. We need an edge against the First Order. Maybe this weapon could be it."

"We do not beat them by becoming them," Rey said,

STAR WARS

anger plain on her features. "Any machine that can make someone do whatever someone else wants, that's not a good thing. That's something evil." She turned to Poe. "You remember what it was like when Kylo Ren took away your ability to fight? Just sitting there, waiting for someone to let you move?" She shook her head. "When I fought Supreme Leader Snoke he stopped me, just stopped me from being able to control my arms, my legs. It was the worst thing I've ever experienced. Why would you want to do that to anyone else?"

"But doesn't it matter how the tool is being used?" Rose asked. "We use blasters just like the stormtroopers use blasters, but we use them to fight for the Resistance, and they use them to build a new empire. And what about the Force? Kylo Ren and Supreme Leader Snoke used the Force to make you both feel helpless, but that doesn't mean the Force is a bad thing. It just depends on how people use it."

Poe stroked his chin as he considered the conversation. "That's true, but I think there are some weapons that no matter how useful they might be, General Organa would never use."

"Like the Starkiller," Rey said.

"Exactly," Poe said. "I think we should figure out what this weapon is first. We have no idea what the Empire was doing all the way out here, and until we do, we should remember our goal: fix the *Falcon* and stop the First Order."

"That's something we can agree on," Rey said. "We can wait until we find out what this weapon is before we decide what to do with it. But for now, I think we should get some rest. It's going to be a busy day tomorrow."

Rose nodded, even though her expression was still thoughtful. But there was no point arguing about it until they knew just what this weapon could do.

And with that final thought, Poe snuggled into the strange purple chair-bed and promptly fell asleep.

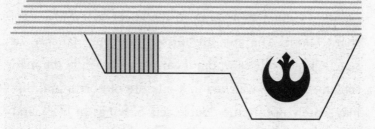

# CHAPTER 15

COMMANDER SPIFTZ was just finishing up his breakfast of nutrient paste when the yelling started. He at first chose to ignore it. Any mishaps could be handled by his subordinates, even if they were all bordering on incompetent. He still had his morning routines to attend to.

But when something tore through the roof of his command tent, revealing pink sky above, and a ferocious scream nearly rattled his bones, he very quickly decided intervention was the better course of action.

Commander Spiftz stormed out of his tent to absolute chaos. Stormtroopers fired into the sky, flamethrowers and blasters filling the air with smoke. Junior officers ran this way and that, shouting orders no one obeyed. For a moment, Commander Spiftz thought maybe the Resistance had launched a preemptive attack, coming for the First Order before he could strike at them.

A creature the size of a TIE fighter swooped past, forcing Commander Spiftz to his knees to avoid razor-sharp talons. The creature missed him but managed to snag a junior officer whom it carried away while the man screamed. Spiftz watched in a mixture of horror and dismay, barely noting the double sets of wings in black and white and the shriek as the thing flew off into the sky.

"What in blazes is happening?" Commander Spiftz yelled.

"It appears we've been sighted by the mekle, Branwayne." Glenna Kip approached, her expedition suit flashing gold and silver as she moved. One of the creatures—the mekle she'd called them—dove at her but then swerved to avoid her at the last possible moment. Commander Spiftz got the impression of feathers and speed before the monster was gone.

"They seem to have an aversion to you," he said, afraid to stand up straight in case another of the mekle came for him.

"The reflective action of my suit discourages their predatory behavior. And honestly, these are juveniles. Full-grown mekle are much, much larger. This swarm will abate once they've gotten their fill." As though to illustrate her point, a nearby stormtrooper was carried off, and then another.

"They are eating my already sparse forces," Commander Spiftz said, watching in dismay as at least a dozen stormtroopers were taken by the mekle, most likely for breakfast.

"None of the useful ones, I hope," Glenna Kip said. Commander Spiftz narrowed his eyes and tried to ascertain whether or not the woman was joking. She did not appear to be.

"Once they've gone we can establish a perimeter of flashing lights. That will discourage them from attacking again," Glenna said, watching dispassionately as a mekle carried off yet another stormtrooper.

Commander Spiftz tilted his head so he could better study Glenna Kip's expressionless face. "And how is it you come by this knowledge, Madame Kip?"

"As a professor, my research reveals much of the lost knowledge of the galaxy," she said smoothly, completely unruffled by his sudden inquiry. "If you would like, I can send you some of the documents I've been perusing. The analysis of the plant life in this sector is simply thrilling."

Spiftz suppressed a shudder. Reading was a waste of his time. He much preferred to have someone just tell him the information. It was much quicker.

"No, thank you, I shall pass. Although, I would appreciate you keeping me company until this . . . swarm, you said?"

Glenna gave a slight smile, almost too slight for Commander Spiftz to even notice it. "Indeed."

"Yes, please keep me company until this swarm abates."

"As you wish, Branwayne."

With Glenna by his side, the hunting beasts avoided the area of the command tent, and after another few minutes they were gone.

The early morning quiet was eerie after the turmoil of the attack, and Spiftz's people slowly came out of their various hiding places to look in amazement at the sky.

"Stop gawking at the sunrise and prepare a defensive perimeter!" Commander Spiftz shouted, startling a few nearby officers. "Flashing lights placed at five-meter intervals to repel the creatures. And I want to know who was in charge of the patrols."

"Lieutenant Glick was, sir," someone called.

"And where is he?"

"Gone," someone else answered, gesturing up at the sky.

Glenna Kip coughed, the sound suspiciously close to a laugh, but when Commander Spiftz looked at her face, it bore no sign of amusement. Not that he'd know how that even appeared in her kind.

"Branwayne, was there some matter you wanted to discuss? Someone left a summons from you in my quarters."

Commander Spiftz gave a quick nod and turned back to his waiting officers and stormtroopers. "Clean this place up, set up a perimeter, and get some heavy cannons prepped in case those things come back."

People scurried off and Commander Spiftz spun on his heel and strode back to the ruin of his command tent. The place was barely serviceable, and he had to push aside a large swath of material that had just moments before the mekle attack been the top of the tent. He offered Glenna Kip a chair, which she politely declined. Commander Spiftz didn't quite know what to do with himself, so he settled for standing a meter or two away from her with his hands folded. After a moment he cleared his throat.

"Last night, one of our patrols ran afoul of the Resistance," Commander Spiftz said. "And it occurred to me that they might also be looking for these lost Imperial laboratories. It is common knowledge that the Resistance is without resources at this point, and discovering a cache of high-tech weapons would help their foolish cause."

"Yes, it had occurred to me that we might not be the only ones looking for this place," Glenna said. "Which is why I took your Lieutenant Nivers with me last night and the two of us found the labs."

Commander Spiftz stared wide-eyed at the woman for a long moment before saying, "You found them?"

"The entrance at least. Neither Nivers nor I could figure out a way in. Branwayne, I sent you all this in my report. Did you not receive it?"

The slight chastising tone of her words made the First Order officer flush. "I have not yet had a chance to go through my correspondence."

"Well, surely Nivers came to tell you herself?"

Commander Spiftz tried to keep his expression bland, to hide the sudden fear that made his pulse thrum in double time. Nivers had withheld the information. He'd never gotten any kind of sense that the girl was ambitious, but if she'd found the labs and hadn't shared the information, well then—perhaps he needed to be a bit more firm with his junior officers. He wasn't about to be outmaneuvered by a lieutenant.

The labs, and the recognition, would be his. He'd worked too hard to let that slip through his fingers.

Glenna Kip, fortunately, seemed unaware of Spiftz's sudden panic. "Well, my suggestion is we call back the teams you sent to find the Corellian freighter—if they're even still alive, one would've thought they'd have returned by now—and turn our efforts towards taking the labs."

"That's a good idea," Commander Spiftz said. He

wasn't quite sure what was happening. He'd awoken that morning firmly in control of an operation, and now it felt like everything was slipping through his fingers. Half his stormtroopers had either gone missing or been taken by monsters, he had no idea which junior officers were assigned to which tasks or whom he could trust, and Glenna Kip had suddenly become more assertive than ever.

He had to take back command.

Spiftz straightened and gave a short nod. "Upload the coordinates to every last person in camp. We're going to take those laboratories and use whatever weapons are there to destroy everyone else on this planet. We leave in an hour." He would make sure he won, one way or another.

Glenna Kip nodded and left the tent without a word.

Commander Spiftz was certain he had only imagined the disapproval in her expression.

# CHAPTER 16

REY STRETCHED AND STIFLED a yawn. For the most part she'd slept well, but their conversation before bed had stuck with her, bringing her restless dreams of battle. As she, Rose, Poe, and BB-8 waited for the Zixon to finish gathering, she was transported once more to the conversation from the night before.

She couldn't help considering Rose's question about what they would find at the labs. If there was some kind of legendary weapon that could help the Resistance stop the First Order, should they take it? Even if it was something very, very dangerous?

Before bed, Rey would've said no. But after thinking about it, she didn't really know what the right answer was. She knew she had to prevent the First Order from getting the contents of those laboratories, but what about after that? What if something in those labs really could help the Resistance?

What then?

"Are we ready?" Lim called finally. Rey pulled her attention back to the task before them. The plan was to head to the area of the tunnels that the Zixon called the Forbidden Lands. Rey wasn't sure how far these dangerous tunnels were from the laboratories, but she hoped it wasn't too great a distance. Lim had warned them as they'd eaten breakfast that the way would be perilous, but they didn't have any other option. The only place they could possibly find a compressor housing to repair the *Millennium Falcon* was the labs, and if they had to pass through these Forbidden Lands to get there, then so be it.

The way was so dangerous that Jem was staying behind. "I have to prepare my people for war with the First Order," he'd said when asked if he was coming along. "Soon we will not be able to hide down here from the stormtroopers, and we must prepare for the inevitable." Rey was sad not to have the wise old Zixon by their side. Very few of the Zixon knew Basic, and Rey had enjoyed the elder's company.

But he had a good point, and his decision to stay reminded Rey that there were much bigger things at risk.

Not that saving the Zixon wasn't important enough, but the whole galaxy depended on just the tiny spark of the Resistance that was left. It was up to them to ignite the flames of rebellion, calling on the entire galaxy to fight to stop the First Order. And although Rey wasn't scared to fight, it was a lot to think about.

As their group moved forward—about twenty Zixon accompanying them, all wearing the same strange bandoliers Lim did—Rose made her way to Rey's side.

"Are you okay?" she asked as they walked, the light of the city dimming the farther they went from the sun tube. "You look worried."

"I've been thinking about what you said, about this weapon that the Zixon told us about. And I'm wondering if maybe we should try to take it back to General Organa and let her decide whether it's something we need or not."

"We don't even know what the weapon does," Rose said. "So it might not matter."

"I feel like everything matters, more and more," Rey said. "Something about this place, something about the work we're doing here, it feels important. Like a turning point."

Rose nodded. "I feel that way, too. It's because we know how bad the First Order is, and how important it is that it's stopped."

"Yes, but it's going to take everything we have and then some," Rey said. "They have so many troops and TIE fighters and ships. We just have us and the *Falcon*, and that needs repairs. We can't even call for assistance! Any advantage we can take, well, we're going to need it with these odds."

Rose pursed her lips and set a hand on Rey's arm. "We will win, because the Zixon need us to. Besides, you're already a hero, Rey! You flying the *Falcon* is worth at least ten TIE fighters."

"Hey, Rose is right," Poe said. "We've got this."

Rose nodded. "I have to believe that things will work out for the better. And I know they will."

"Of course they will," Poe said, BB-8 beeping in agreement. "We just have to take it one step at a time. That's all you can do when things start to feel impossible. Take it one step at a time and make the best decisions you can."

BB-8 gave a series of happy beeps, and Poe laughed. "Yes, Beebee-Ate, you did teach me that. Thanks for pointing it out."

They fell silent as they entered the tunnels. The Zixon arranged themselves in a formation known only to them, taking the front and rear of the group and putting the rebels in the middle. BB-8 rolled around, weaving around the Zixon, who swatted at him and chirped in annoyance.

"Beebee-Ate, I think you're distracting them," Rey said, unable to hide her smile. BB-8 let out a series of mournful beeps, and Rey shook her head. "Those were children you were playing with last night. These are warriors. They have work to do."

They moved through the tunnels quietly after that. The tunnels turned and twisted, and the more they walked the more a sense of foreboding fell over Rey. The tiny hairs on the back of her neck rose, and she pulled her staff from its holster. Rose and Poe pulled out their blasters, as well.

"You feel it, too?" Rey asked, voice low.

Poe nodded. "It feels like we're being watched."

"These are grobel tunnels," Lim said. "We must be very careful."

They walked a little farther, and the sensation of being watched grew so strong that Rey wanted to scream. She was just about to ask what these grobel looked like when a roar echoed through the tunnel, shaking the ground and rattling her bones.

"Grobel!" Lim shouted, and the Zixon readied their weapons. A thumping noise came from farther down the way, and when the creature was within a few meters Rey finally saw why the Zixon feared them so.

The grobel filled the tunnel, and Rey figured these things, not the Zixon, must've made the tunnels. The grobel had a long body that seemed to be covered in gem-stones and a round mouth that was nothing but teeth, each one longer than Rey's arm. As it pulled itself through the tunnel with two small appendages, the stones on its body ground against the tunnel walls, chipping away any rocks that got in the way. On Jakku, Rey had once polished a bit of metal until it shone like a mirror, and she figured the stones on the grobel's body did something similar to the tunnels. Rey had no idea how the thing knew where it was going, though. The creature had no eyes.

"Quickly, this way," Lim said, and they ran down a side tunnel that Rey hadn't seen until Lim pointed it out. A few of the Zixon launched bags of a sparkling powder at the beast, which made it roar in agony and back up a small bit. As it did, a stormtrooper's helmet fell from between the creature's teeth.

"I think Sparkles there already had dinner!" Poe yelled.

"Then let's not be dessert," Rey called back.

"Can't we just blast it?" Poe asked, running along beside Rey.

"Blasters do not work on the grobel," Lim said, manag-ing to keep pace with the much taller humans. "The beams are reflected back. Shooting at the grobel is a very bad idea. Only the xinda flower dust can keep them away."

They ran until Rey's side hurt and she was afraid they'd

be lost forever. The plants that lit the way changed from orange to blue to green to purple, and still they ran. Rey glanced over her shoulder, looking for the grobel, but as far as she could tell, the way was clear.

Finally, Lim signaled a halt. Poe, Rose, and Rey all bent double, gasping for air. Of the twenty or so Zixon who had begun the trip, fewer than ten remained. BB-8 beeped mournfully, and Rey nodded.

"Beebee has a good point. Where'd everyone else go?"

"They're leading the grobel away so we can finish our trip," Lim said. "Do not worry about the warriors. We have fought the grobel many times. They are vicious but easily tricked." Her whiskers twitched with pride. "My warriors will return to our side when it is safe. Come, let us not waste any more time. We are nearly there."

Rey tried to put her worry aside, but she was only partly successful. She still worried about the other Zixon, even if they were experienced fighters. The grobel had been terrifying, and she wouldn't want to have to face down such a massive beast. The creature reminded Rey of the rathtars she and Finn had once run from, only with fewer arms. Just as many teeth, though. She hoped their new friends were safe.

The tunnel turned, and suddenly their group stood before a giant metal door. A few of the Zixon froze, even going so far as to take half a step back. Lim turned and chirruped at them, but they would not be moved.

"This is the door to the Forbidden Lands. I will go with you, but they will remain here."

"This looks like a research facility of some kind," Rose said, wrinkling her nose in confusion.

"Maybe it's the labs," Poe said, eyes widening. "It could be that the place the Zixon call the Forbidden Lands is the research labs the First Order is looking for."

Rey watched as a few of the Zixon turned their backs on the metal door, their chattering language sounding more and more concerned. "I think you're right, Poe. The Forbidden Lands are the lost laboratories."

"They're afraid? Is there a reason? Like, are there more grobel on the other side of this door?" Rose asked, looking a bit uncertain herself.

"My warriors are uneasy because they remember the days before. This is a place of sadness and loss for us," Lim said, her whiskers drooping slightly. "But you will find what you are looking for inside. There is a place our friend called a hangar in there. It is a place for flying machines, yes?"

"Yes," Rose said. "A hangar should have the piece we need."

Lim's whiskers perked up a bit. "I am not so afraid of this place, and I brought our friend here before so that they could get equipment." Lim hesitated. "But I will not leave my warriors alone this time. I will remain with them."

Rey nodded. "We understand and appreciate you helping us get this far."

Poe and BB-8 stood near the door, studying it. "How do we get this thing open?"

"Look," Rose said, going to stand next to Poe. "There's some kind of keypad here."

"Lim, do you know how to open the door?" Rey asked.

"I do not, friends, I am sorry," the Zixon replied before turning back to her very nervous warriors.

"Beebee, can you give us a hand?" Poe asked.

The droid rolled left and right before the door, giving it a good once-over. There was a socket just a little way below the pad, and BB-8 connected to it. A short while later, the door began to move, rolling back with a scream of metal and a groan of gears.

The light streaming from inside the room beyond made the rebels shield their eyes and blink. Rey wiped away tears caused by the sudden brightness, but she could see that what lay beyond was a stark contrast to the tunnels. White tile floor stretched into a room that was like nothing else on Minfar. The lights were daytime bright, and beyond the first room Rey caught sight of a stairwell, a giant lift, and more space beyond.

The Forbidden Lands were indeed an old laboratory.

Rose's eyes went wide, and she walked inside. "Look at all of this! I haven't seen anything like this since I left home." Wires spilled off of workbenches, and various bits of debris here and there gave the impression of great works unfinished, machines abandoned before completion. Glass walls divided the space into multiple work areas. One space was overrun with dead plants, their experiment long since ended, and another contained blasters of varying sizes, all half assembled. There were a handful of stormtrooper helmets tossed into one corner, blackened and charred like someone had spent a lot of time pointing a blaster at them.

"Do you think this was an Imperial laboratory?" Rey asked.

Rose pointed to a sign, which advised all members of the lab to update their process logs often. "That looks like the Empire's official seal right there."

"Rose, do you want to see if you can find a compressor housing upstairs?" Poe said. "It seems like the hangar would be closer to the surface, especially if this place was built according to Imperial plans. Rey and I will check out the rest."

Rose nodded and ran off toward the lift, BB-8 following.

Rey walked behind Poe as they began to explore, taking

more time to linger over the leftover equipment. There was a salty-soo, the nickname for a desalinization pump, and over on another table was an ion booster. Rey couldn't help calculating how many portions all the labs' leftovers would fetch back on Jakku.

The Forbidden Lands were a veritable goldmine.

The place was large enough to house all of the Resistance, but that wasn't saying much. Still, the Empire had managed to build an enormous laboratory on a far-off planet that few people had heard about. Rey had already understood why the First Order must be stopped before she saw this place, but realizing just how powerful the Empire had been only strengthened her resolve.

"Lim," Poe called, turning back to the door where the Zixon were clustered nervously, still mostly in the doorway but creeping closer in tiny increments. "Do you know where the weapon you told us about was kept?"

"It was right here, but we've gotten it already," someone said.

A line of stormtroopers and a First Order officer stepped from the shadows, blasters pointed at the rebels. Poe and Rey exchanged glances before raising their hands in surrender.

"Well, what a delightful surprise. Rey, I believe it is? Supreme Leader Kylo Ren will be very happy to see that

I've claimed you as a prize." Before Rey could comment, the man dismissed her and turned to her companion. "And the famed Poe Dameron." He stalked toward the pilot. Rey didn't recognize the man, but there was no mistaking the First Order uniform.

Poe frowned, hands still raised. "Yeah, that's me. Do I know you?"

"I am Commander Branwayne Spiftz of the *Ladara Vex*," the man said, preening as he talked. "And now I am also the man who captured two of the heroes of the Resistance."

"Not quite!" came a shout from the back of the lab. The ground shook, rattling lights and causing a few of the stormtroopers to drop to their knees. At first Rey was afraid the grobel had returned, but then she saw what was causing the commotion.

The lift in the rear of the lab lowered and suddenly dropped a massive machine, shaking the building and sending Rey into a crouch. A pod hung suspended between two huge metal legs, like some kind of hunched creature. Inside of the pod sat Rose, each of her hands gripping a control stick. On either side of the pod, like arms, were blaster cannons. Rose grinned as she turned the cannons on the stormtroopers.

"Surprise!" she said, launching a barrage of cannon fire at the troopers.

The First Order scattered, and Rey ran along the opposite wall toward Rose and her machine as the stormtroopers returned fire. Poe ran alongside her, his expression jubilant.

"Is there another one of those?" he asked, ducking a piece of flying debris.

"Let's hope so!" Rey said. She ran in the direction Rose had come from, but she wasn't the only one. A couple of stormtroopers were on her tail, and Rey slid to a stop and drew her staff while Poe pulled out his blaster.

A stormtrooper tried to climb the leg of the walking cannon Rose piloted, and Rey made quick work of him with her staff, hitting him upside the head so he fell to the ground in a heap. Most of the First Order were fleeing, heading back the way they'd come, and the cannons Rose fired after them filled the lab with smoke so it became harder and harder to see.

"We have to get that weapon!" Poe called.

Rey ducked through the smoke, trying to fight her way to the First Order officer they'd seen. But even though the stormtroopers were no match for her staff, Rey couldn't get close enough. She watched as Commander Spiftz had an animated conversation with a tall, willowy woman dressed in flashing gold and silver. Whatever they were arguing about was soon concluded, and they both spun on their heels and left.

The stormtrooper in front of Rey suddenly turned and ran, and Poe poked his head up over the desk he'd taken cover behind. "Why are they leaving?"

"They still have the weapon," Rey said. "They're probably trying to escape with it."

The door of the walking cannon opened, and Rose jumped down. Black smoke billowed from the pod, and she held a bag that Rey didn't recognize. "Well, that thing is done. Experimental, but seriously fun. Anyway, I found a ship I could scavenge for the *Falcon*, and a whole bunch of other equipment besides. With this I should be able to fix the engines," she said, pointing to the bag. "But first we have to stop the First Order. You saw what this thing can do! That weapon they have, who knows what they'll do with it."

Rey nodded. She couldn't imagine the weapon in the hands of someone like Kylo Ren. "Let's get back to the *Falcon* first. Trying to go after them now could be risky. Hopefully, once we patch up the engines and repair the satellite we can send a message. I think we need some help."

"Well, then, let's get out of here!" Poe said.

Poe, Rose, Rey, and BB-8 all sprinted toward the door they'd entered through. But when they got there, all the Zixon were gone.

"Where are they?" Rose wondered aloud.

"Look!" Rey said, pointing to where the First Order was retreating down a side hallway. Lim and her warriors were right with them, running along in between a couple of stormtroopers. At first Rey thought the stormtroopers were kidnapping the Zixon, but then she realized that the stormtroopers weren't even pointing their blasters at Lim or her warriors. And there was no way the Zixon would have gone along quietly, either. They would've fought as much as possible, especially against stormtroopers.

Rey tried to run after Lim, but the stormtroopers turned their blasters on them, firing at Rey so she had to duck behind a large metal crate. When she poked her head up over the top of the crate, the First Order was gone.

And so were the Zixon.

"Why did they do that?" Rey asked as Rose and Poe ran up. "They were our friends."

"Did you see their ears and whiskers?" Rose asked, her eyes wide. "They looked sad."

"The weapon," Poe said. "That commander must have turned it on during the fight. He must've summoned them to his side. That's why they weren't fighting."

Poe was right. Perhaps that was what the commander and the tall woman had been talking about. Who was she? She hadn't looked very happy about what was happening.

Rey holstered her staff and looked toward the other end of the lab in the direction the First Order had gone.

"We have to save Lim and her warriors. And stop the First Order here. And we have to do it before they can escape with that weapon."

"Well, let's see what else could be useful here besides this walker," Rose said, going back to the great metal beast and climbing back in. "If we're resourceful, we can figure out a way to maximize our assets."

Rey nodded, putting her sadness aside. She stood taller. "Luckily, scavenging is one thing I know how to do," she said with a wry grin.

They were going to save the Zixon. Rey could feel it.

The First Order would be sorry they ever came to Minfar.

# CHAPTER 17

GLENNA KIP LOOKED AT the assembled Zixon in dismay. They followed Commander Spiftz as he marched through the jungle. Their whiskers were slack; their eyes stared straight ahead without any kind of real acknowledgment of what was going on around them. It was just like the last time, but also worse.

Because this time it was Glenna's fault.

When she'd first met the Zixon so long ago, she'd found the small creatures odd. They'd been curious about the lab, funded by the Empire and full of so many humans. Glenna and her team had been researching how sound could be used to subdue unruly populations. It had been awful work, but she'd been young and alone, her planet destroyed long before she'd hatched.

She'd somehow thought that by working for the Empire she could stop them from doing anything too terrible or creating weapons that hurt too many people.

She had been wrong.

When the Empire fell she'd been the first to free the Zixon from the power of the Echo Horn, even though she knew she'd waited longer than she should have. It was a shame she'd carried with her for a very long time, but she was not the same person she'd been back then. This time she wouldn't hesitate.

There was nothing she could do for Lim and her warriors at the moment, though, so Glenna fell back into the group of stormtroopers, waiting until they were no longer paying attention to her before slipping into the cool shadows of the jungle.

Glenna had an excellent sense of direction, and her kind had once hunted their prey on the open prairies of a planet that no longer had a name. So it was with little effort that Glenna ran through the jungle, heading back toward the labs. She was faster than any human, and very soon an entrance to the labs arose from the jungle.

This was a different door than the one she'd tried to enter the night before, but just like the other door to the laboratory, this one rose up out of the ground, a strange, seamless black wall of shiny rock with no discernible entryway.

If she was lucky the Resistance would still be there, and she could follow them back to their ship. Somehow, she would have to convince them that she was there to help, not hurt.

She'd nearly made it to the door when a droid came speeding out of the entrance, beeping directions to the people who followed. Glenna scaled a nearby tree, leaping from branch to branch until she could peer down.

"It looks like we're the only ones here," said a male human with dark curly hair. Poe Dameron, Branwayne had called him. His companions appeared by his side, and the three conferred in low voices, too quiet for Glenna to hear.

Below her, the astromech droid buzzed up to the tree she perched in, sensing her presence. She froze, waiting for the droid to give her away, but it just rolled off, bumping along the ground.

"Great, it's decided then," said one of the other humans, this one with pale skin and straight black hair. "There are entirely too many stormtroopers to stage a rescue with just the four of us. We at least need the *Falcon* up and running. Let's get the ship flying first, and then we'll rescue our friends."

The droid beeped in acknowledgment and rolled off through the jungle, the people following it cautiously. Glenna waited for them to get farther ahead, and then she began to follow, leaping from tree to tree so the rebels wouldn't know they were being tailed. When the time was right, she would reveal her presence. But first she needed to figure out a way to convince them that she was on their side.

And then they could crush the First Order together.

# CHAPTER 18

ROSE CROUCHED IN THE UNDERBRUSH and swatted away a particularly annoying bug. A little way away, crowded around the *Millennium Falcon*, were several stormtroopers. They blocked the entrance to the ship and were generally doing what all stormtroopers did, which was ruin her day.

She really, really wished she'd been able to bring the mechanized walker with her from the labs. Those blaster cannons had been very effective, and it was pretty fun to operate. Maybe if there was time later she could sneak back to the labs and take the machine for another spin.

But they had to take care of the stormtroopers first.

"Do we have any ideas?" Rey whispered, gesturing in the direction of the ship.

"We could shoot them," Poe said.

"There's too many," Rose said, panic starting to rise. She firmly pushed the feeling aside. She could panic after they'd found a way back on board the *Falcon*. Until then, she was going to focus. There had to be a way for them to get rid of the stormtroopers. "Maybe the porgs could help? I bet they're inside."

"Or those stormtroopers ate them," Poe murmured to himself, but Rose heard.

"They better not have," she began, but never got to finish her threat.

From nowhere, a silver blur appeared. Three of the stormtroopers fell, and the rest shouted.

"Hey! What was that?"

"No idea. Be ready."

"It's over there!"

The stormtroopers turned and fired, pointing away from Rose and her friends.

"That's our chance!" Rose said, leveling her blaster at the stormtroopers.

"But what happened to those first three?" Poe wondered aloud.

"We'll figure it out later," Rey said, pulling out her blaster, as well.

The rebels fired stun blasts at the stormtroopers. The

First Order soldiers were thoroughly confused, and they fired at both the jungle and each other without quite understanding just what they were shooting at. It was all over very quickly, leaving the stormtroopers splayed out on the ground.

Rose, Poe, and Rey quickly disarmed the stormtroopers. Poe ran inside the *Falcon* to find some rope to secure the enemy soldiers, and while he was gone a woman slipped out of the jungle in a metallic suit, her hands held high.

"Please do not shoot," she said.

Rose grinned. "You knocked out the stormtroopers!"

The woman nodded. "Yes, I am here because I need your help. I figured if I helped you first you'd be more likely to help me."

"Help you do what?" Rey asked, her posture defensive. "You were with the First Order back at the labs. I saw you."

The woman nodded, and Rose's happy feelings melted away. This woman was working with the First Order, and nothing good came of anyone who would work with them. For a moment Rose remembered DJ, the thief she and Finn had met on Canto Bight. She'd thought he could help them, but it turned out he was only interested in helping himself. There was no use trusting anyone who didn't know the difference between right and wrong, because eventually they'd end up selling you out to some storm-troopers. Rose was still mad about that.

"I agreed to help them find the Echo Horn because I wanted to destroy it, but I was unable to get to it before they did. And I was not counting on the labs being full of the Zixon. I didn't want them to get hurt."

"Maybe you shouldn't have helped the First Order at all. Because your plan apparently stunk."

Poe walked down the boarding ramp, his blaster pointed at the woman. "Rose is right. If you're here to help the Zixon, why were you working with the First Order?"

The woman's shoulders sagged a little. "They came to my lab after the destruction of Hosnian Prime a few months ago and offered jobs to everyone there. Those who refused were killed. I didn't have much choice. When another First Order officer began to talk about the labs here I knew it would only be a matter of time before they discovered Minfar's secrets. I decided I would use the First Order to find and destroy the Echo Horn and Minfar could take care of the rest." Something close to a smile altered her expression, even though it was more a hint than an actual grin. Her lips were so thin that they were nearly nonexistent.

"You're a scientist?" Rey asked.

The woman nodded. "And someday I will tell you the

story of how my team designed the Echo Horn and used it to enslave the Zixon, a terrible event that I regret. But now is not the time. I take it your ship has been disabled?"

"Oh, we just have to replace the compressor housing and the engines should be fine."

"Good, because we don't have much time. A large contingent of the First Order is set to arrive on the morrow, and it would be best if we could rescue the Zixon and destroy the Echo Horn before reinforcements arrive."

Poe put his blaster away and nodded. "Can't really argue with that."

Glenna lowered her hands and gave a quick nod. "All right, then. Let's get your ship fixed up. And after we do, I'll tell you what I have in mind."

While Rey and Rose fixed the engines, installing the pieces of the compressor housing and then powering up the *Falcon* to ensure everything was working correctly, Glenna and Poe rounded up the stormtroopers and tied them to a tree. Rose walked down the boarding ramp just as Glenna and Poe returned from their final trip.

"Are they going to be okay out in the jungle?" Rose asked, thinking of the grobel they'd seen in the tunnels. She didn't like stormtroopers, but it seemed rather mean to tie them up so they could be eaten.

"They'll be fine until we free the Zixon. After that, we

can worry about what to do with them," Poe said. "I mean, they might get eaten," he admitted at Rose's startled look.

"They will be fine, even though they do not deserve your mercy," the scientist, Glenna Kip, said. Rose wanted to ask the woman where she was from and how she'd come to Minfar so long ago. She seemed to know a lot about the planet, and Rose had so many questions about the plants and animals there. But as Glenna had said, there wasn't time for that just yet.

"Where's Rey?" Poe asked.

"Trying to call the rest of the Resistance on one of the secondary backup channels," Rey said, walking down the boarding ramp to stand next to Rose. "It might be good to get some help. We have no idea what kind of forces are here."

"The *Ladara Vex* is a light cruiser, and it shouldn't be a problem. It's a smaller ship, still bigger than your freighter here, but we have an easy way to get rid of it."

"How's that?" Poe asked.

Glenna Kip smiled just a little. "I've been building a mini reactor in my sleeping quarters on the ship. I told Commander Spiftz it was a device to locate some of the lost tech down here in the labs, but the truth is it's really a bomb connected directly to the power systems of the *Ladara Vex*. As long as I can get back on board, we can destroy it from the inside."

Rose couldn't help laughing. "That's brilliant. You really weren't here to help the First Order."

"No, I was here to help the Zixon. If we can retrieve the Echo Horn and destroy the *Ladara Vex*, we can hopefully get a few of those delightful ships we got from Aftab Ackbar on Mon Cala in place for an ambush."

Rose's mouth fell open, and her shock was echoed on both Rey and Poe's faces. BB-8 beeped something that sounded like surprise, as well.

"How do you know about those ships?" Rey asked.

"I have worked very closely with General Organa for a long time. I've been communicating with her as best I can, but until recently I have been very closely watched. There are some things in the labs, more honest weapons than the Echo Horn, that could help the Resistance even the odds against the First Order. I couldn't get away from the First Order to find them myself, so I used their resources to bring me here. I figured it would be more useful to spend some time aboard a First Order cruiser. It gave me time to slice some codes and research their locations."

"You're a spy!" Rose said.

"I am a scientist," Glenna corrected, "who sometimes spies. The First Order really did come to my labs, so I had no choice but to work for them."

"But it didn't mean you were actually helping them," Poe said.

Glenna inclined her head in agreement, and a feeling of relief came over Rose. With allies like Glenna, smart allies who could make the best of a bad situation, the Resistance would soon be more than just a tiny spark.

It would be a flame, a beacon of hope for anyone who saw the First Order for what it was and was brave enough to step forward and fight. Rose stood a little straighter and felt glad that they'd come to Minfar. This was what being a rebel was all about.

"So, should we go save our friends?" Rose asked, and everyone nodded. BB-8 chirped and beeped happily before rolling around in a circle.

"All right, then," Poe said, nodding. "Here's what we'll do. . . ."

# CHAPTER 19

COMMANDER SPIFTZ looked at the assembled group of Zixon and smiled. They stood at attention, waiting for his next command, oblivious to anything but him.

They were the perfect little green, fuzzy soldiers.

"Remove the flashing beacons around the perimeter and replace them with new ones," he said, and a group of the furry creatures darted off to comply with the command.

It was absolutely brilliant.

Commander Spiftz had been expecting a weapon of some sort in the labs, a cannon or an untested walker like the one that Resistance woman had turned against him and his stormtroopers. That the Echo Horn was a small box was an unexpected surprise.

Small, yet so powerful. Mighty enough to change the course of history.

Commander Spiftz couldn't wait to show off the device to the First Order high command. The box, no bigger than a blaster, with only a single button and a series of knobs, had completely enthralled the local populace when he'd turned it on. A weapon like that could be used to conquer an entire planet, assuming one of the First Order scientists could figure out how it worked. So far, he'd only been able to get it to work on the Zixon. But imagining the larger possibilities for the weapon made him giddy. Turn on the box, tell everyone to lower their weapons, and restore order throughout the galaxy. Or even better, command them to serve you, to answer your every beck and call. It would be even better than being an emperor.

Instead of giving the device to the First Order, he could keep it for himself. Branwayne Spiftz could stay on Minfar and rule the entire planet. That way he wouldn't have to risk sharing his amazing discovery with some scientist who might turn on him at any moment. After all, Glenna Kip had gone running off into the jungle at the first opportunity. He had a small contingent of stormtroopers looking for her, but he doubted they would find her. There was something odd about the woman that convinced Branwayne he had seen the last of her, and any other time he would have been rather annoyed at having been so obviously played for a fool. But that day? He didn't mind as much.

He had the Echo Horn. He was going to become a legend.

But first he had to find the Resistance. Especially that irritatingly good-looking pilot, Poe Dameron. Once he'd captured them, he could deliver them to the First Order and do whatever he chose. Hidreck and the others didn't believe the legendary weapon existed in the first place. It would be nothing to pretend the mission had been a failure and that Glenna Kip had been a Resistance spy he'd had to neutralize to protect First Order interests.

It was everything he'd ever hoped for.

Lieutenant Nivers walked over, her gaze skipping over the Zixon uncertainly. "Um, sir, we have a problem."

"Of course we do," Spiftz sighed, watching as the group of Zixon he'd dispatched to repair a warning light returned from resetting the beacon. "Can you not see I am in the midst of an experiment?"

Nivers frowned, her expression somewhere between displeased and horrified. "I think this might be more pressing, sir. The team assigned to guard the *Millennium Falcon* hasn't reported back. And the team we sent to follow up on them is missing, as well."

Before Commander Spiftz could respond, the *Millennium Falcon* flew overhead, low enough that he could feel the residual heat of the sublight engines.

"Well, there it is!" he yelled, temper fraying. So close, so close to victory, and now this. "Call the *Ladara Vex* and scramble the fighters. It's one ship. There's no reason it should be giving us this much trouble!"

Nivers scrambled off, and Branwayne strode back to his command tent. No matter what happened, the Resistance could not get ahold of the device. That was his key to a brilliant future.

The Zixon milled about, getting underfoot and generally being in the way, and Commander Spiftz pointed to a nearby storage tent. "Get in there right now!" They complied without any response, whiskers drooping, expressions slack. Once they were out of the way, Commander Spiftz hurried to a nearby transport, startling a junior officer standing inside. Spiftz clutched the Echo Horn tightly, refusing to let go of it for even a second. He would have to figure out how to use it on humans, but for now he just needed to get away from Minfar.

"Once the TIE fighters are scrambled, take us back to the light cruiser."

The junior officer shook his head. "Umm, sir, I can't fly this. I'm not a pilot."

Commander Spiftz stared at the man before shoving him out of the way.

"I'll fly it, then," he said.

It seemed as though he was once more going to have to do everything himself.

# CHAPTER 20

**P**OE WAITED UNTIL Rey and the *Millennium Falcon* had the full attention of the First Order before he made his way into camp. Beside him like a metallic shadow was Glenna Kip. The scientist, deadly efficient, felled the stormtroopers who crossed their path, without a sound. Poe watched in amazement as she leapt in the air, delivering lightning-fast kicks to the stormtroopers' helmets, knocking them out before Poe disabled their blasters. Poe wondered what Glenna was planning on doing after she destroyed the Echo Horn. She'd be a fantastic full-time spy.

And the Resistance could use all the help it could get.

Poe waited for Rey to zoom by once more before

running full tilt for a nearby storage tent. He'd watched as the Zixon filed into the space just a few moments earlier, and when he ducked inside it was a relief to find Lim staring back at him.

"Lim! Are you okay?"

The Zixon's whiskers twitched, but she didn't answer. Glenna Kip entered the tent behind Poe, shaking her head.

"They won't be able to answer you. The device limits their ability to communicate."

"What can we do?" Poe asked. He hated to see them like this, so very different from just the day before, when they were dancing and welcoming him and his friends to Minfar. Instead, their whiskers drooped, their shoulders sagged, and their eyes stared sightlessly. This weapon was worse than he'd imagined.

There was no way the Resistance could use something so awful against people, not even the First Order.

Glenna looked around and pointed to a nearby transport shuttle. "We have to get the device from Spiftz."

Poe took a deep breath and let it out. "All right, let's go."

Glenna led the way, running and ducking as the stormtroopers turned their attention from the *Millennium Falcon* and turned their blasters on her. Poe ducked behind a supply container and fired back at the stormtroopers, but he was only one person and there were at least a dozen of them, all firing in his direction. Poe was pinned down. He reached into his pocket and withdrew a communicator.

"Rey, can you hear me?" Poe said into the small device.

"Yes, what's going on?"

"The First Order commander is escaping with the Echo Horn. We need to get rid of it before the Zixon will return to normal. Can you stop that transport ship?" A little way off, a boxy ship of the sort used to transport stormtroopers lifted off, clearly headed back to the *Ladara Vex*, which Glenna had told Poe was still in orbit over Minfar.

"Maybe," Rey said.

Just then, a handful of TIE fighters appeared, flying overhead. Poe's heart sank as he looked at them. There was no way Rey could fight those ships and stop the commander from escaping with the Echo Horn.

"Poe," Glenna Kip said, appearing next to him and startling him badly. "You need to get a ship and stop Branwayne and the *Ladara Vex*."

"How am I supposed to do that?" he asked, ducking to avoid being shot by the stormtroopers. Glenna pointed toward another of the square transport ships that the First Order used to fly short distances, this one parked nearby. It was not exactly what Poe had in mind when someone talked about flying. In fact, just the thought of trying to maneuver the slow-moving craft through the blaster fire all around them made Poe a tiny bit nervous.

Poe *really* missed his X-wing.

"When you get on board, find my quarters at the rear of the ship. The device I rigged is connected to the power lines of the cruiser. It looks like a droid in need of repair. You'll have just enough time to get off the ship before it explodes."

Poe nodded. As Glenna returned fire he ducked behind the supply crates until he was close enough to get onto the ship. BB-8 rolled on board as Poe darted inside, mashing buttons until the bay doors of the transport closed.

"All right, let's see if we can manage to get out of here in one piece."

Poe strapped himself into the pilot seat of the transport, fired up the engines, and launched himself after the fleeing First Order officer.

# CHAPTER 21

**R**EY SAW THE SECOND transport ship taking off. She had just enough time to turn the *Millennium Falcon* toward the escaping shuttle before the first TIE fighter fired on her.

"Rey, we have company," Rose called.

A porg landed on the control console near Rey, and she waved it away. "I see them. Can you see the shuttle? We have to stop them from getting away," Rey said.

"We have bigger problems right now," Rose said. "We need to handle those fighters before they handle us!"

"I'm going after the Echo Horn, Rey," Poe said over his comlink. "You make sure that those fighters don't have a chance to figure out I'm not just some scruffy First Order moof-milker running for home."

"I'll try my best," Rey said. "I'm going to try to lead them away from you." She turned the *Falcon* toward the TIE fighters, six in all, and took a deep breath. "Are you ready, Rose?"

"We can do this!" Rose yelled back from her position in the gun bay.

And then the TIE fighters were on them.

Rey yanked on the yoke and twisted the ship around as two TIE fighters closed in, their cannons letting loose a punishing barrage. Rose returned fire with the ventral gun, but the shots went wide, missing the enemy ships.

The TIE fighters' assault was much more successful, and Rey gripped the yoke as the ship shimmied and shook from the cannon fire. The porg in the cockpit screamed and lodged itself in the space under her seat. Rey couldn't really blame it. Things were about to get interesting.

"Rose, hold on, I'm going to try something."

"Go for it. Anything is better than this. Ugh. Stay still!" Rose said as another TIE fighter sped past.

Rey took a deep breath and closed her eyes. All this time she'd been trying to reach for the Force, the spot inside of her that felt more connected to everything. Again and again it had been for naught, and she'd gotten more and more frustrated.

But this time she relaxed into the warm potential of

the Force and she asked it to guide her, to make her steady, to lead her on a path that was successful. She wasn't a Jedi, and she was nothing like Luke Skywalker, but for a moment Rey sensed something—a spark of possibility, an inkling of potential—and she felt more centered and infinitely more capable.

The Force was all around, just as it always had been, but this time Rey could feel it. And within that source of energy, she asked for help from Minfar.

When she opened her eyes, she still saw the TIE fighters. She also saw a flock of the giant creatures that had attacked them on their way to Minfar, approaching at a very high rate of speed.

"Um, Rey, are you seeing this?" Rose asked.

"Yes. Don't worry about them, just focus on the fighters," she said. She couldn't have explained why, but she felt like the creatures were there to help.

"Hey, do you see the company you're about to have?" Poe cut in over the comlink.

"It's okay, Poe. We've got this!" Rey called.

One of the winged creatures forced a fighter to the ground, the ship exploding in a fiery cloud. "Hey, I guess these giant flying things are here to help!" Rose yelled.

"Yes! I'm going to take us into this canyon up ahead. Hold on!" Rey called.

She yanked hard on the yoke, forcing the *Falcon* into a steep dive between two pillars of rock. Rey's heart pounded as she negotiated the *Falcon* into a canyon. The sheer walls sped by, a blur of red-and-black-striped rock, and most of the TIE fighters dropped back, only two ships following them into the treacherous twists and turns.

"Rey, it looks like we lost most of them," Rose said, voice hopeful.

"Let's hope our newfound friends are taking care of them."

The closest fighter let loose a volley of blaster fire, and Rey flipped the *Falcon* at just the right moment to avoid the blasts. They hit the side of the canyon instead, causing a massive landslide of rocks and dirt, a chain reaction that began to run the length of the canyon, more and more of the canyon wall crumbling as the *Falcon* flew past. Rey pulled on the yoke and the ship rose, just barely missing the nearest falling boulders.

"Um, Rey? How stable is this place?"

"I see it, Rose. It gives me an idea."

As Rey negotiated the twists and turns of the canyon, she began to work through the possibilities. "Rose, when I give you the signal, I want you to shoot at the canyon wall."

"Are you sure, Rey? That seems pretty dangerous. I

mean, you're a great pilot, and I can totally make the shot, but there are so many rocks, and if we don't shoot at the right time we're going to be grobel chow."

"Rose," Rey said, unable to hold back a smile. "We can do this."

Rose took a deep breath and let it out, the sound echoing through the intercom. "Okay, just tell me when."

Rey continued to pilot the *Falcon* through the twisty terrain, avoiding the nearly constant cannon fire from the TIE fighters on her tail. Her palms were a bit sweaty and her heart thrummed in her ears, but she had to wait until just the right moment, just the right spot.

"Now, Rose!" Rey yelled as they passed a huge outcropping. "Aim for that skinny spot in the middle." The arch of stone had a narrow piece about three quarters of the way down on the right-hand side, and a well-placed shot would bring the whole thing tumbling down.

Rose fired several times at the spot, and Rey held her breath as they flew past, bits of stone pinging off the top of the *Falcon*. At first, Rey thought the TIE fighters were too close, that the outcropping would take too long to fall. She wondered if maybe she should try using the Force to move the giant rocks. After all, she'd done it before back on Crait.

But then the entire mass of stone began to fall, smaller

rocks and then bigger ones as the entire outcropping crumbled. Rey swung the *Falcon* up out of the canyon and back around just long enough to see the TIE fighters getting pummeled with rocks before being buried completely.

"Woo-hoo! It worked!" Rose shouted.

"Yes, and it looks like our friends took care of the rest of the ships." On the ground the wreckage of the other three enemy fighters smoked, their center pods cracked open and their side wings in pieces.

"What do you think happened to the pilots?" Rose asked.

"I'd rather not think about it," Rey said with a grimace.

"Hey, that was some amazing flying, Rey," Poe cut in across the comlink. "You really are something else. The Resistance is lucky to have you."

Rey grinned. "Well, it's all up to you now. Rose and I are going to head back to clean up the rest of the First Order. Make sure you stop Commander Spiftz from leaving with the Echo Horn."

A crackle of static answered Rey as Poe flew out of range for the comlink, but she wasn't worried. Poe could handle himself.

They were the Resistance, and the First Order was about to learn never to underestimate them.

# CHAPTER 22

POE MANEUVERED the transport into the wide landing bay and tugged at the First Order tunic he wore. Finding an officer's uniform on the transport had been very good luck; he just wished it fit a bit better. The top cut across his broad shoulders a little, digging in so that if he had to raise his hands over his head it would be very uncomfortable.

Here was hoping that wasn't an issue.

BB-8 beeped his concern, and Poe shook his head. "No, you stay here. We're going to need a way off this ship before it blows. Make sure no one but me gets into this transport. Can you do that?"

BB-8 beeped an agreement and Poe stood straighter, like a self-important First Order officer might, opening the bay doors to the transport shuttle to exit the boxy gray ship. As soon as Poe stepped into the *Ladara Vex*'s hangar bay, BB-8 shut the shuttle door. Anyone who walked by would have no idea the little droid was even inside.

Poe walked toward a doorway that looked to lead to the rest of the ship. He kept his blaster holstered even though he would've appreciated having its reassuring weight in his hand. It just wasn't something a First Order officer would do while on board a First Order cruiser.

But as he walked through the halls of the *Ladara Vex*, Poe began to realize that getting caught wouldn't be a problem. The gleaming black hallways seemed to be completely empty. There didn't appear to be anyone on board, and he only passed a single droid, which completely ignored him as it went about its duties.

This was going to be the easiest mission ever.

Or maybe not. Glenna had said her rooms were in the rear of the ship, but now that Poe was on board he wasn't exactly sure where that was. There were doors aplenty, and they all looked exactly the same. The ones he opened revealed a kitchen mess and a lounge, but nothing that looked like the rooms of a scientist. And it wasn't like he could ask someone walking by.

The sound of voices echoing down the hallway forced Poe to duck into a nearby alcove.

"I cannot wait until Commander Hidreck gets here. Spiftz has totally lost his mind. Did you see that thing he brought back from Minfar? Does that look like some kind of legendary weapon to you?" They were two First Order junior officers, each of them pale and tall. One had brown hair while the other was blond, and both of the men looked annoyed and upset.

Poe pressed into the shadows of the space, holding his breath as the men passed. But he needn't have worried. The two junior officers were so involved in their argument that they didn't even notice his presence.

"You'd better be careful with what you say. For all you know the commander is monitoring our conversation," said the blond man, looking around guiltily as though he expected Commander Spiftz to jump out of one of the many rooms they passed.

"But it's just a tiny box! I bet it doesn't even work off of the planet down there. It doesn't make sense that we spent so much effort trying to find that thing." The other First Order officer, his dark hair cut incredibly short, gestured wildly as he spoke, oblivious to his blond companion's obvious concern.

"Look, pipe down. The last thing you want is Spiftz mad at you. Who knows what he's capable of."

"You're right. Let's go search this scientist's rooms and

get back to the command deck. This place kind of gives me the creeps with everyone gone."

The blond man put a friendly hand on the dark-haired man's shoulder. "It could be worse though. You could be eaten alive by something on Minfar! We were lucky to get to stay on board."

The voices moved past Poe, and he waited a couple of heartbeats before stepping out into the hallway after the junior officers. He followed them to the rear of the ship, and as he was drawing his blaster, one turned around.

"Hey!" he yelled just as Poe shot him, the blaster bolt knocking him out. Poe didn't give the other officer a chance to draw his blaster, and once both of the men were unconscious Poe opened the door to Glenna's rooms and dragged them inside.

"Okay, if I were a bomb built by a hyper-intelligent scientist, where would I be?" Poe muttered as he began to poke around the room. He was beginning to despair. Neither the bed nor the refresher nor the dresser revealed anything. Then he opened the closet and paused. Inside was what looked to be an astromech droid, a larger model than BB-8 but smaller than R2-D2. But when Poe poked the droid, it was clear there was something off about the thing. Poe lifted the top of the not-droid and saw a series of flashing blue and green lights inside.

"Yes!" he said, giving himself a moment to celebrate. There was nothing so obvious as a switch, but when he pressed one of the lights, the entire panel went red and an automated voice said, "System armed. Five minutes to detonation."

"All right, time to get out of here."

Poe turned to leave and stopped short. Standing in the doorway to the room, his hair disheveled and his uniform a mess, was Commander Spiftz. He looked as though he'd just been through an ordeal, and Poe wondered what had happened to the man. He held something in his hand, but Poe couldn't see what it was.

"Poe Dameron. Have you come to turn yourself in?" Commander Spiftz asked, straightening his uniform and smoothing his hair.

"No, not exactly," Poe said, giving a sheepish grin. "I've come to destroy the Echo Horn, and your ship, as well."

"Well, that is rather unfortunate," Spiftz said, holding up a small box. "Because instead you will end up my slave. Kneel."

Poe lunged for the device, but Spiftz danced backward and mashed a button on the side. The First Order officer's expression went from triumphant to confused.

Poe didn't know what Spiftz had been expecting, but the small device had no effect on him. He drew his blaster and fired at Spiftz, knocking the man down. Poe hesitated, wondering whether or not to take what must have been the Echo Horn.

But it was only a momentary hesitation, and instead of taking the destructive device along, Poe stomped his foot down on the box, smashing it to smithereens.

"Blast!" yelled Spiftz. He grabbed Poe's ankle, and the Resistance pilot tried to kick him away before losing his balance and falling to the ground. Spiftz pulled at Poe's hair, and Poe responded by punching Spiftz. It was a good punch, and the First Order officer fell backward, completely unconscious.

"Sorry, friend, I have places to be," Poe said, fixing his hair and uniform.

And then he ran full tilt for the hangar bay, wasting no time getting away from the ship before it blew.

# CHAPTER 23

COMMANDER BRANWAYNE SPIFTZ woke slowly, realizing that something was very wrong. For one, he was lying on the floor. For another, the Echo Horn was lying a few meters away, smashed to pieces.

"No," Branwayne said, sitting up with a wince and reaching for the device. All his work, all his effort, for nothing.

And he'd let the Resistance get away.

Branwayne got to his feet and ran to the command deck. Poe Dameron had said something about destroying his ship, but he wasn't beaten just yet. The *Ladara Vex* was small enough to fly into a planet's atmosphere. He would just have his officers take them to the planet's surface. He would blast the entire surface into a crater, that way when Hidreck arrived he'd at least have made some progress. Sure, his own officers and stormtroopers would die, but it would be better than admitting he'd been fooled by Glenna Kip and he had not a thing to show for his little adventure to the edge of space.

But when Spiftz arrived on the command deck, he found it empty. Not a soul remained on the *Ladara Vex* but him, and on the monitors he watched as a timer counted down to zero. It took him a long moment to realize what it was, but he needn't have wondered long. When the time ran out a hologram appeared on the command deck.

"Hello, Branwayne. This is Professor Glenna Kip. If you are watching this, you are finished. This is just the beginning, by the way. The Resistance will not be stopped. It cannot be stopped. But you?" The hologram smiled.

Branwayne didn't even have time to regret the things he'd done. Not that he would have, anyway. "Rebel scum," he muttered.

It was the last thing he ever said.

Commander Hidreck and her Star Destroyer came out of hyperspace outside of Minfar's ice ring, not long after the destruction of the *Ladara Vex*. Every alarm on the command deck began to howl, and the junior officers operating the terminals began to push buttons frantically, sending out queries to the various sensors that provided input.

"What is that?" Commander Hidreck barked, gesturing to the debris floating before the observation window.

"Ma'am, it appears to be the remnants of the *Ladara Vex*. It's been destroyed."

"How? There are no viable threats in this sector!" Hidreck said, incredulous. Had that fool Branwayne Spiftz actually run afoul of the Resistance? The scouts she'd sent to this sector had reported nothing but empty space, no other fighters in sight. She refused to believe she'd been wrong. She had followed protocol to the letter.

But just then a small fleet of ships flew out of the ice ring around Minfar. Hidreck watched in shocked dismay as they began to wipe out her smaller ships, cutting a deadly path toward the command vessel.

"Scramble the fighters! Battle stations!" she cried. Leave it to Branwayne to downplay the danger so he would look like a hero.

Commander Hidreck alerted high command to what was happening, but soon after, her ship joined the debris field around Minfar.

# CHAPTER 24

REY, POE, AND ROSE watched as the Zixon finished rounding up the remaining First Order soldiers. Glenna Kip and Jem were in deep conversation. Rey smiled, her heart light and glad and a sensation of righteousness leaving her a bit giddy. They'd managed to stop the First Order, destroy a light cruiser, and liberate their new allies. Other Resistance members had ambushed a First Order Star Destroyer just moments earlier. It was a job well done, and so much of the fear she'd felt just a couple of days before melted a bit.

They could do this. The Resistance could defeat the First Order. It might not happen in a single battle; it might take a long time. But as long as they remembered what mattered, taking care of people from all kinds of places, they could win this war.

They could keep hope alive.

Glenna Kip and Jem walked over, and Glenna bowed to the rebels. "Thank you so much for your help. Without you, the First Order would've been able to use my device for ill, and my guilt would continue to grow. This is the first time I've felt free in a very, very long time."

"The Resistance exists to help people, to make sure that everyone has a choice," Poe said, and BB-8 beeped in agreement. "By the way, have you ever thought of becoming a spy? You are very . . . resourceful." His cheeks flushed a bit. "We could use someone like you on our side full-time."

"The Zixon, too," Rose said. "The fight against the First Order is going to be long and difficult, and we're going to need all the help we can get."

"I do believe a few of my warriors would like to accompany you on your adventures," Jem said, whiskers twitching as he stood a little taller. "We've been fortunate to keep the First Order from gaining a foothold here on our homeworld, but we know there are others who have not been so lucky. We should help them gain their freedom, as well."

"Perhaps the Resistance should consider a recruiting location," Glenna said, her expression thoughtful. "I would be happy to help you identify some options. My travels through the galaxy have been extensive, and there are many planets like Minfar that the Inner Rim has forgotten."

"That's not a bad idea," Rey said with a nod. "But for now, we have to get going. We still have to deliver these supplies, and I'm certain that General Organa will be waiting for us to tell her the complete story of what we've gotten up to."

BB-8 chirped mournfully, and Rose laughed. "Well, I don't think we're going to be in *that* much trouble. Everything turned out okay, after all."

"Thankfully," Rey added.

"But we'll be back soon," Poe said. "We still need to see what else is in those labs that the Resistance can use!"

"And you will need to come back to visit some of your friends," Jem said, pointing to the group of porgs that had begun nesting in the trees nearby.

Rose frowned. "I don't know if it's such a good idea to leave them here."

"Don't worry. Minfar's ecosystem will take care of them before they can get out of control," Glenna said with a kind smile.

BB-8 beeped happily, and Rey laughed. "Beebee-Ate is right. Don't worry, Rose, there are still plenty more of them on the *Millennium Falcon*." Rey turned back to Glenna and Jem. "We definitely need to come back, if only to see how

the porgs fare on Minfar. Oh, and be kind to your First Order prisoners." A group of stormtroopers, their helmets removed and hands secured behind their backs, walked by led by one of Lim's warriors.

"Oh, we will," Glenna said with a nod. "Lucky for us the labs have a very nice cell block where they can stay until we decide what to do with them."

"We will treat them better than they deserve," Jem said solemnly.

Rey, Poe, Rose, and BB-8 waved goodbye as they headed back to the *Millennium Falcon*. Their hearts were light, and even though there would be tough battles ahead, they could celebrate.

But tomorrow? Tomorrow they would continue the fight.